BRE GARCIA

The Jackrabbit's Ofrenda

A Jackrabbit Brujo Tale

1

Vel pulled his safety glasses up and rested them on his forehead, squinting at the squad car parking outside his house. Lieutenant Kulasiewicz, rigid and stone-like as always, stepped out and started up the driveway to him.

"Aw hell, Lieu, why didn't you tell me you started taking house calls?" he greeted with humor. The sky was clear and the mid-September sun bright but not harsh. Though it was still warm, the promising chill of autumn hid in the spaces where the sun couldn't reach. Lieu's eyes were shielded by sunglasses, but Vel saw her mouth move with a sigh of exasperation and he smiled.

It was funny how change had a smell even if it was hard to quantify what that smell *was*. Mid-September smelled like—but not exactly—the air before a storm. It felt like—though not exactly—the gentle steam from a watched pot readying to boil. Both things and all things related to it were so much easier to feel when looking back on them. That's how Vel came to keenly know change—only after it had started. Some of it was manufactured in his brain, such as how his final words to his mother became damning. Those words tormented him because they had come to signify change when previously they were too mundane to be so. Others, sharpened in the moment. The night his beloved Laura was killed he recalled how the refrigerator's idle noise cut through everything else and made the house feel horribly empty. At the time he attributed it to simply missing her like a dumb dog.

But he should've been listening more carefully and heard it for what it was: incoming loneliness forecast by the rattling queries in his kitchen. *Is there anybody out there? Hello? Echo, echo, echo. Where did you go?*

Why isn't there someone else here?

There was one thing that never changed, and that was Lieu. Other than making house calls. He cocked a smile at her for it, not that she could tell what he was thinking.

Lieu stood firm in front of him. Vel, shirtless, coated with sweat and sawdust, was sitting at the mouth of his garage. Just behind him was a circular saw and a messy pile of wood. His car was parked out in the driveway to make room for it, and his bike hung unused from the ceiling. Moreover, he had let his curly hair grow long enough to be pulled back in a ponytail as it hadn't been since his teen years. The hairband he used was one of Laura's, with a woven pink and red pattern. At some point he'd wander in to have it cut to its regular moppish length. For now it served as evidence of his emotional stupor. Lieu's mouth twisted in maligned curiosity and she raised an eyebrow at him. Vel reached for his water bottle and drank as she explained herself.

"We got a call for some suspicious and or indecent behavior at your address."

"Well now that's not very nice," he said with a gasp, screwing the cap back on. Sure his body wasn't much to write home about, but it certainly was interesting to look at. Six-seven, scrawny enough that his elbows could be registered as weapons, huge hands, and an oddly broad swimmer's chest when the rest of him was branch-like—weird for sure, but not *indecent.* Of course, the concerned caller might've been influenced by his copper skin, knowingly or not. But just as he steadied the rosary on his rearview when the cops pulled him over, he paid it no mind and pretended it was normal, "How much time do I have before your knights crest the hills and take me by force?"

Exasperated, Lieu quite clearly rolled her eyes from behind her sunglasses, "It's just me, Vel."

"Damn. It was getting boring around here."

"Is that what you call this," Lieu leaned in to peer at the saw. Vel reached over and pulled two pieces of wood from the pile.

"You know how things look super easy on paper and then you try to do 'em and it sucks?"

Lieu watched as he aligned the pieces of wood, the 45 degree angle he cut into the corners matching up well enough. But behind him was a ridiculous growing pile of ridiculous scrap wood, just an arm's throw away.

"What are you doing?" she asked, and for once didn't sound like a cop about it. Vel handed her the pieces then used his long arm to reach back. Shaking the sawdust off of the photo, he showed her Laura's smiling face. From there the attempts at a picture frame became clear.

"Laura's dad insisted I pick up a new hobby. *His* hobby. Then lent me some of his toys. It's going uh...," Vel shrugged, "Well, it's going." It was something, at least, to help him wade through the misery of losing her.

"All you seem to have done is cut pieces." Lieu commented. Unspoken, she was questioning how cutting angled lines could be hard.

"It's not *right.* I don't know, something just isn't right about one piece or the other." From years of making the odd trinket with stones, bones, and leather, he knew when things felt *correct* in his hands. The wood just wasn't correct and it was close to driving him mad.

Though, he was more than a little afraid of screwing up. The pendant he had made Laura had twisted and deformed a man into a beast. True, he could very well see how the pendant merely revealed that man's inner self more than transformed him. But it cost Laura her life. Untrue, but Vel couldn't shake the guilt. Now, he didn't think he risked anything like *that* with a mere picture frame—maybe. He didn't know, and with his mother long gone he had no one to ask or guide him. All he knew was be careless with baking and you got dense inedible mush. Be careless with magic and people wound up dead. That was the fear.

Even though she was already gone.

Vel sighed, defeated. It had been a long summer. Longer when he thought back on it. Longer when he stared at the scrap wood piled where Laura's Jeep used to be parked.

"You aren't here for a case, are you?" Vel ventured to ask, wary. Though part of him missed work and every day he felt closer to being able to return, the prospect of jumping in without warning was frankly anxiety-inducing. At some point he'd have to brave it, but not now. Not while her picture frame was in pieces.

"No. Just a wellness check."

"From what you said that's a helluva wellness check." Vel frowned.

Lieu pulled her lips back in reluctant agreement, "Hence why I sent myself and not someone else."

Something struck him in the chest at those words. He was

often at odds with Lieu over nothing more than a clash of personalities. She was practical, he wasn't. She was stern, he was loose. She was by the books, and when that didn't work she called him in to work his magic. The glue that had set between them that made such a relationship possible was nothing short of miraculous. How she trusted him, why he trusted her despite being worlds apart in mindset and occupation—occasionally she was blunt about it and it caught him in an old and buried place.

Errant barking interrupted them. He peered around his car to see the dumb, smiling face of a bully breed tromping up to his garage. Her owner was behind her, a real dad's-dad of a retiree with tight neon sports clothing and skin that was impossible to tell if it was burned or tanned. Vel often overheard his wife scolding him for not putting enough sunscreen on, though it seemed rooted from a loving over-precaution rather than his stubbornness. He had a cheerful cute accent and, like all the other retirees in Tucson, was from somewhere up north and snowy. Dave Reed was his name, his wife's was Barb, and their dumb-happy dog was Miss Daisy. Vel didn't know them that closely, but he chatted with them enough to know that Dave referred to her walks as *walking Miss Daisy*, followed every time by a laugh at his own joke.

"Now Miss Daisy! Just because I loosened the leash doesn't mean you gotta go barking up every tree you see!" he scolded without reprimanding her, then greeted with a smile, "Howdy, howdy!"

"Heya Dave," Vel returned with achingly mellowed energy. Taking a moment to put the guard back on the sawblade, he reached down to where Miss Daisy was licking his shin to rub her velvety ears, "That's not a bone, girl! Or at least, not yet it ain't."

"There isn't any trouble here, is there officer?" Dave asked as Vel fetched a plastic bowl from further back in his garage, nudging it in place with his foot before pouring the rest of his water in for Miss Daisy to lap up, "Vel's a sweet kid."

Vel took the opportunity to give Lieu his biggest bluest puppy eyes, "He called me sweet."

Lieu sighed with the full knowledge that Vel would never let her forget that, "No. We just got a call for suspicious behavior."

"I'm suspicious?" Vel pouted at her.

"Suspicious behavior?" Dave raised his voice, aghast, "Well who the hell called ya? Don't tell me it was Paul across the street!"

"That's, uh," Lieu began but Dave was already set off. It started with how crazy old Paul was, then launched into the first anecdote of Paul rearranging the rocks on their lawn because he found them ugly. Then Paul yelled at his wife for being seen in a bathrobe to check the mail. Then, on and on every transgression that had been catalogued of old Paul's nastiness. From there, he started the next anecdote about a neighbor two doors down—related only by the merest threads.

The best part was that Vel sat there and said nothing, letting his stories ramble on with Lieu in unfortunate attendance. It was only when Miss Daisy had drained the bowl and started licking his shin again that he interrupted to snap Dave out of his babbling.

"Don't you worry about me, Dave," Vel said with a grin, "Lieutenant Kulasiewicz and I go way back. Did I ever tell you about the time she put me in a jail cell then decided to let me out because I was such a sweet kid?"

"*Vel*," Lieu admonished harshly, "Spare me the details of

something I was *there* for. I came in for a check-up *only*, not to chit-chat."

"Sure, Lieu," he patted Miss Daisy's neck, pursed his lips, and looked up at her, "And Miss Daisy has more than one brain cell."

Dave laughed raucously, a noise that made Lieu shift on her feet in agitation. He finally called his dog away and bent down to nuzzle her nose-to-nose, "All that empty room for extra heart cells!"

With a good-bye that was light on its feet, Dave left. Vel watched him return to his house. Lieu recovered in the resulting silence.

"...Laura liked the neighbors here, a lot." Vel remarked, his voice weak and his vision blurring.

"Undoubtedly." As always, her words could've been twisted as mean or cold. Maybe it was meant as such. But Lieu only ever said what she meant.

Vel kicked the water bowl off into the corner and stood up, stretching to his full height, "Better a situation than I ever lived before."

Lieu paused, "...Yes."

She remembered. Vel smirked. It was hard to forget, but it was good she remembered. Even with the nasty neighbor and the double-takes that had followed him throughout his giant life, he wouldn't go back to the small trailer-like home with his tía. But he'd remember.

"By the way," he said, still mellow and not quite his usual self, "I'm heading to the border at the end of October."

"The border," Lieu echoed, curt and vaguely suspicious.

"Yeah. Haven't been in a while. Want to see it again." Vel spoke casually but he couldn't deny the strain it took to talk about it, "Mind coming with me? Don't want to get deported."

"You won't get deported." Lieu said firmly, matter-of-factly, like he could be dumb for fearing so, "It's illegal."

Vel puffed out a breath. Lieu was well aware of the dissonance between reality and law, but that didn't stop her near-dogma attachment to the written ideal. He didn't want to get into it now.

"That's a yes, then." He said it as a statement, and correctly too. Lieu gave a small nod, leaving without another word.

Vel stared at the pile of cut wood, contemplated, then started sorting through it instead of cutting more.

2

Dom had been large for as long as Vel had known him. Breaking six foot by the eighth grade and pear-shaped in his fatness, he was a reject alongside motherless, stick-figure Vel. They were loyal rejects, playing tabletop games at lunchtime despite the stains on their character sheets. Dom wrote and directed well, and Vel always considered him contemplative and creative. After Laura's death he had reached out several times, but it had taken until the turn of the seasons for Vel to finally make good on the offer and appear for a game again.

Saint that he was, Dom didn't mind, and Vel felt his visage crack when engulfed by his warm arms. He knew how to hug right. The only thing that kept him together was Dom's young daughter, Izzie. Six years old and bouncing off the walls to see her Tío Vel for the first time in months. For her sake, or perhaps for Vel's, Dom didn't mention Laura.

The evening belonged to them and their old games; familiar, warm, and good. Izzie sat in Vel's lap, chaotically ruling her character in ways her father guided (though sometimes he super-ceded her own story for the betterment of the campaign). She didn't mind—maybe wasn't aware that it was happening. She was simply happy to be there, even though Vel knew his lap was not comfortable to sit on. It was a good distraction. It was a good way to crawl back to the world.

The later it got the more Izzie slumped, then suddenly their game was far quieter with her snoozing against Vel. Dom's voice was soft and Vel's to match, rolling dice on a flannel shirt placed on the table so as not to wake her. Vel watched the mismatched colors roll until his vision blurred.

He blinked and glanced down at the growing weight in his lap. His mind played terrible tricks on him, chit-chattering in his ears. Remember how she had felt as a newborn? Hot and small and dwarfed by his big hands? Dwarfed more still when Dom held her? And funnily enough she was growing into playing dwarves for their campaigns. Remember how the hospital felt when rushed through, laughing heartily when newborn Izzie screamed—remember how Laura smiled with love, because it had become clear to her that she had chosen a good man to date? Remember, painfully remember, the burning spark that perhaps one day Izzie would have a lifelong friend in his own child. Vel's eyes stung. Adjusting her carefully so she wouldn't slide off under the table, he suddenly realized that he hadn't spoken for several minutes. Dom had said nothing either, scratching notes down while a gnat flew around the dining room light.

"Dom...," Vel said, staring at his friend's daughter. The scratching pencil paused. Vel sucked in a harrowed breath and finally told him what he had told no one else, "Laura was pregnant."

His friend looked at him properly, and Vel couldn't decide if he could meet his gaze or not. Dom's face was kind. Under the overhead light his eyes were big and horrified, his frown sympathetic and accented by his beard. Vel raised a hand to start rubbing tears away.

"I...," he choked.

Dom turned towards him, scooting the chair closer. The question he said may not have been the most tactful, but it was surely the only one that came to mind in the moment, "How long?"

"I, I don't know," Vel choked again, "She hadn't yet told me."

"Vel...," Dom said, solemn. There was a moment where it seemed he was going to reach forward to hug him again, but his eyes dropped to his daughter and he hesitated. His look deepened in sorrow when it went back to Vel. Babysitter. Uncle. Best friend. It hadn't been a pressing priority for Vel to have children with Laura. Maybe it should've been. Maybe it *shouldn't* have been. Vel knew what it felt like to lose a parent, particularly a mother. He didn't wish that on anyone. Maybe in the end it was a blessing.

It didn't feel like one.

Dom swallowed hard. Vel finally looked at him, eyes red and chest staggering on every breath.

"Six weeks. Eight, maybe." he guessed. Dom's eyes screwed shut and he pressed his fingers to them, shaking his head. Izzie stirred in Vel's lap and drew her father's attention, who reached for her despite her sudden protests.

"Bedtime for Izzie Lee," he announced softly.

"*Nooo*," Izzie blearily whined, "*Daaad*,"

"Story's done for the night," Dom said, lifting her until she pressed her cheek against his shoulder. Vel mustered a smile and waved at her, following Dom to her bedroom.

"Promise?" she asked sullenly, unconvinced.

"Promise-promise," Dom said.

Vel nodded in turn, "Tío Vel's gotta go back into his hole."

"But you'll be back, right?" Izzie asked, her eyes suddenly sharp for how sleepy she was. Piercing. Drilling for an answer, because it had been *so long* since she had last seen him. A few months was so much more of her life than his, after all.

"'Course I will. But only if you go to sleep."

Vel watched from the doorway as Dom tucked her in—tighter than he remembered him doing before—and kissed her forehead good night. He tried not to look awkward or sullen. More than anything he hoped that such things were too complex for Izzie to pick up, or if she did she didn't understand it enough to realize what was going on—that anything at all was going on. He backed out into the hallway as Dom quietly shut the door then jerked his head to the front of the house.

Soon the two of them were on the front porch in the midnight air. Vel dug out a cigarette and lit up, Dom watching him without saying anything. It's not that he'd lecture that it was a bad habit, it was the implication that Vel was back to smoking at all. Not one cigarette throughout the entirety of his relationship with Laura, and now it was his routine again. He paused, palm against his forehead, wanting to start the conversation but finding his throat coiled up. Dom remained silent. That made it worse. Vel started sniffling, curling his lanky body tighter over itself.

Then it happened. A flooded dam, a burst, and Vel quietly sobbed. It wasn't fair that Laura had been murdered. She had been his life. Beyond that he had a house now because of her, had finally felt financial stability with her help—and now, morbidly, off her life insurance. Seeing Izzie had been as healing as it gouged the wound wide open. Part of him wished he hadn't known at all, but he only had his own snooping ass to blame for that. Even if that led him to the killer in the end, it hardly felt worth the extra pain.

Dom let him cry, the same way they had let each other cry on the eve of high school graduation. Every now and then he struggled to say something, to explain himself, but Dom knew well enough. Vel had loved Laura with his whole heart, and Vel's heart was oversized to begin with. Had to be, to reach his toes. *Chose* to be, because he kept losing people left and right.

Shaking, Vel took a long drag of the cigarette as he tried to calm down.

"Been a while since this," his voice wavered, tilting his head back to blow straight up, "Just sitting and shooting the shit."

"Less time to do nothing," Dom mused, "Izzie Lee starting first grade, Hannah nabbing that promotion while my contract runs dry, no wonder adults were so high-strung."

Vel laughed through his nose, "Funny, I feel like I've been doing jack shit for months on end now but still just as high-strung."

"Well...," Dom said, leaning back on the porch stairs, "Feels like graduating high school all over again I guess."

"Better," Vel said after a bit, "and worse, at the same time." He put the cigarette to his lips and sucked in. Both men fell silent, letting Tucson fill in the gaps.

"...Sebbie would've loved this campaign, Dom." Vel said, staring up at the cloudless stars.

"You say that after every session." Dom quietly snapped.

"Am I wrong?" he shot back, "You get better at writing Alburin every time too."

Alburin, Sebbie's elf bard. Flamboyant, confident, funny, and sweet. Yet for all those descriptors Dom winced and tucked his expression into his hat, almost as if in shame. Vel frowned, but the answer came soon enough.

"I get better at writing how he was in high school. But people grow up and change and how they write changes too—I've gone back and reread some notes from campaigns we did only two years ago and winced. I'm not better at writing Alburin, I'm better at writing what Alburin *was*. Not how Alburin would've changed, not how Sebbie would've—,"

"Dom," Vel interrupted, "Jesus. Sebbie doesn't hate you."

"That's not what this is about, man,"

"The hell it ain't," Vel said gently, cigarette flopping in his lips, "'Else why do we always got an empty chair at the table?" Izzie knew not to sit in it. Hannah knew not to sit in it if she ever wandered into their campaigns.

"...I don't know," Dom said after a while, "It just feels nice to believe he's there."

Vel looked out across the dark street and all the porch lights both lit and unlit, the desert brush scuttling with nocturnal lizards and rodents. Over the nearly thirty years of his life Vel encountered, re-encountered, and further encountered the dead. First his mother when he was twelve, then his best friend Sebbie when he was seventeen, lately Laura at twenty-eight. Dotted and littered in between them were all the murder cases Lieu had called him out to consult on solving, dead body after dead person rolling in front of his eyes. It was familiar, it was agonizing, it was his job, it was his life, it was his grief. He wasn't quite used to it even after all this time, and more than that he still didn't know what to make of the spirit after life. His mother had been accused of being a bruja and he believed there to be truth in that statement. He took to her practices with some stride, offering weird but palpably doable private investigations as a career.

And still, he only ever believed spirits to be where he wanted them to, instead of *knowing* they were there. Did Sebbie sit across from him every tabletop session, or was the chair only seating dust motes? He didn't know. He wanted to comfort Dom and say that it was true, but the only thing he could muster was that it was right to believe. Moreover, that it was right to keep the chair empty. Even if it was only for their comfort.

"Vel," Dom offered, his own eyes shining in the light, "I am so, so, so sorry about Laura."

"I know you are, softie," Vel weakly jabbed. After all, Dom wasn't the one months-deep into a depression he was only just starting to crawl out of. Well, maybe. Crawl around was more accurate, "...Thanks for having me."

"Thanks for saving me from packing all my books into the car and driving to your house to force a session."

"*God*," Vel swore, "Thank fuck you didn't. You don't wanna see how it's been, man."

Dom shrugged, "You gotta clean it sooner or later. Which, by the way, what are you doing for Día de Muertos?"

"That an invite?" Vel puffed, "Thanks. Sorry, spending it with my tía." It was a sweet gesture on Dom's part, but Vel wasn't quite ready for Dom's huge family all crowded in the same house. They were lovely, jovial people, and thus far too much for him right now. Granted he and his tía had their spats, nigh relationship-ending ones, but it was more familiar than a sea of faces that multiplied every year.

Dom eyed a car driving down the street, "So long as you do something with it."

"Yeah, I dunno. I got plans this year. It's...y'know. A year for it." Vel said, watching Dom's wife pull up into the driveway. Dom grunted in agreement.

Waving cordially with the cigarette in full view, Vel greeted her, "Heya Hannah. Sorry I stunk up your husband."

"So long as it's just him," Hannah replied, pulling her purse up to her shoulders and shutting the car door, "Then he can deal with it."

Vel chuckled, but he would never smoke in front of Izzie. As far as she knew, the smoke had just become a unique cologne. Okay, maybe she wasn't that dumb. But if Vel could pretend that the ghost of his friend sat in the chair across from him, then he could pretend that his niece-by-oath thought better of him.

3

Vel ran his thumb over the bumps of wood glue, satisfied. The satisfaction sat light in his chest, aired out and content like a brisk morning. Once the glue was sanded smooth along with the rest of the frame he'd start thinking about what to actually carve into it. That felt like something a professional would know *before* starting the project, but for as clumsy as it was Vel was stumbling through the process without a pause. Days had passed, he was pretty sure it was October by now, and there was only a month left.

As such, he was changing the makeshift ofrenda into a proper one.

Constructing a tier with some of Laura's books she'd kept from school (the thick *Canterbury Tales* copy she had served him the best), Vel dug out his baby blanket, smoothed the creases, and laid its bright pink and green colors over his desk. Already it looked less like a slightly organized investigator's den and more like an altar. He set his mother's photo on the high tier, Sebbie's painfully small school photo beneath it to the right, and, well, he laid the work-in-progress frame to the other side. Vel tried to visualize without visualizing it. Good enough. For now he placed an opaque glasses case beneath his mother's photograph.

Within were the lasting remains of her body—not ashes, but her eyes. Potent, magical, sacred to him, and not to be used lightly. He had come to inherit them directly from her dead hand, keeping them secret over the years. She had been his first dead body.

Sebbie had been his second.

Vel's eyes drifted to the creased and faded photo. He always lamented, hurt, that he didn't have a better picture of him—forced to salvage from scraps as Sebbie's family seemed to wick themselves of his existence. He looked just as Vel remembered, albeit frozen in time, albeit never aging. His face was soft and so was his nose, with pale freckles dotting all over. Despite having braces in middle school his overbite still pushed his front teeth out when he smiled. It was less obvious in the photo as Sebbie had started to grow wisps of a mustache to make up for the fact that alopecia had taken nearly half his head at a mere seventeen years old. He had that teenage look about him where he was still soft on some edges but outgrown on others. Like Vel and Dom, he was a reject. But just for a moment in that senior photo his big, bright eyes shone, light brown and enthusiastic. As he should be remembered. School was more a haven for him simply because Vel and Dom were there, and it was at school he could show his enthusiasm without punishment.

No, that wasn't true. As time went on school got worse and worse for Sebbie, and no clinging to his friends lessened the bullying nor the lack of support from home. For those last semesters that he was alive, Vel and Dom lined up their schedules so that at least one or both of them shared a class with him. Vel in particular remembered nabbing the art classes, something he treasured since he got to watch Sebbie draw while he struggled to match his skill.

God, what a year. Vel nudged Sebbie's photo an inch so that the light didn't look as harsh on him, then left the room as his memories took hold.

* * *

Fatty, Cripple Kid, and The Fag. Didn't sound like a half-bad band name, not that Vel caredthat much about music. Fatty Dom was the writer, Fag Sebbie was the artist, and Vel was—well, he was the Cripple Kid. It was a bit of a misnomer; his doctor asserted his body would be tip-top shape once puberty was over. Though he still wore his knee braces he at the *very least*—thank the merciful god Hail Mary and all that nun shit—did *not* have to wear his back brace anymore. Walking through the halls of high school when the braces on his body made just about as much noise as his steps was a nightmare, and what was worse? They really did nothing for the short-term pain. From fifteen to seventeen his body ripped itself apart, growing a foot within a year and then some in the outlying months. Vel was just bracing (pun unintended) himself for when *Orangutan* would replace *Cripple Kid* in the lexicon of his oh-so-fellow students.

Vel slammed his fingers across the strings of the acoustic guitar. Did he know how to play? Fuck no. It was his tía's, undoubtedly used to sing Catholic songs of praise about Jesus and Mary and blah blah *strum strum, strum!!*

"¡Jeró!¡Cuidado con mi guitarra!"

"Huh?" Vel tipped his head over the back of the couch he was splayed on, shouting with a dull tone that played dumb, "Sorry, don't speak Spanish!"

He could *hear* his tía heat up as she whipped around to face him directly, yelling, "¡*Cuidado*—!"

Nope. Vel slammed on the guitar strings again, riffing hard and loud to drown her out. Vaguely underneath his ungodly chords he heard her sigh in frustration and a shit-eating smirk crawled up his cheeks. His one-man trash symphony was interrupted by hergrabbing the neck of the guitar and wrenching it away from him.

"Jeró," she tiredly scolded, "Shouldn't you be doing something?"

"I *was* playing the guitar," he snipped, stretching petulantly with his feet on the coffee table. Actually, he realized, his feet were reaching all the way*across* the table. Without knowing his father, there was no telling how tall he was likely to get. Not to mention that kids sometimes outgrew both their parents. It would've been a fun mystery if it weren't for the fucking braces.

His tía rolled her eyes and pulled the guitar out of his reach, "And your homework?"

"It's Friday," Vel pointedly protested, standing up. Often she didn't make a fuss about homework for most of the weekend—unless he was annoying her, "I'm gonna go pick Sebbie up for a movie night at Dom's."

At that, her eye turned scrutinizing. In a shallow way—she knew and didn't mind his friends but there was always that twinge of suspicion that he was up to no good. Apropos of nothing, of course! That was how he saw it.

"And where are you going?"

"To the video store to pick stuff out, Dom's handling the food and snacks and drinks—,"

"What *kind* of drinks?"

"*Sodas*, Tía Gloria."

"Cuida tu tono, do you know what they can put in sodas?!"

As if rum and coke was a subtle name at all.

"Cocaine, probably." Vel casually offered as a much worse alternative—which, predictably, nearly set her off again.

"Jeró,"

"Oh come on, Tía," Vel huffed, "It's just gonna be a night at Dom's, like last week and the week before that!" He could go on about how they don't drink either, and if they did it wouldn't have been the hard stuff put into soda, for chrissakes. As a former nun *chrissakes* was her least favorite phrase, and wanton use of it would shift her focus to chewing him out over that rather than the fact that he admitted to having drunk alcohol not under her supervision. But before he launched into that trick his tía's face warmed and she reached up to place her hands over both his cheeks.

"Mi buen hijo. Staying out of trouble and doing the right thing." she cooed, rubbing his cheeks like he was a baby.

"Yep," Vel said, dropping his hand to his back pocket, "That's me." Keeping his eyes fixed on hers to watch her expression change, Vel pulled out a cigarette and placed it in his lips. The warmth turned to blunt shock as she watched him pull *her* lighter out of his other pocket to light up right in front of her.

"¡¡Jerónimo!!" And thus followed a string of enraged Spanish as Vel clamped his teeth on the cigarette, turned heel, and bolted out the door. His tía was in hot pursuit, clawing at the air just behind him.

"Be back tomorrow morning Tía bye love you!" Vel chirped, slamming his car door shut and racing out of the driveway. On cue, one of her chanclas hit his side mirror and Vel flinched, cackling with glee as he sped out of her range.

As he drove, the houses turned from cramped and rundown to well-groomed with maintained yards. That didn't mean green lawns, but it did mean nice colorful desert plants set in the center instead of sparse shrubs eking out at the sides. Vel parked in front of Sebbie's house, a nice two-story family home in a nice family neighborhood. Quiet, reserved, and Vel honked his horn twice to break the silence.

It wasn't long before Sebbie emerged from his house, walking quickly but not too quickly, not like he was excited or anything—because his mother was trailing behind him. Swearing, Vel snatched the cigarette out of his mouth, snuffing it on the armrest before frantically hiding it in his pocket. Sebbie remained calm and coolly unenthusiastic as he opened the door and slipped into the passenger side of the car. His mother, holding her elbows in a standoffish manner, bent down to look Vel in the eye. Putting on his best smile that was wide enough to show the gaps between his upper premolars and canines, Vel greeted her in his best, most *professional* tone.

"Afternoon, Mrs. Moore."

"Mr. Velasquez," she said, cold and with suspicion.

"It's just Vel, Mom," Sebbie protested quietly, but she acted as though she didn't hear him.

"Where are you going?" she scrutinized.

"Dom's house, for movies."

That was the correct answer since it must've lined up with what Sebbie had told her. Reluctantly she straightened up to bid them good-bye and Vel carefully drove down the street.

The second he turned onto the next one Sebbie burst and Vel did too.

"*Shit*, do you think she smelled the smoke?!"

"Oh my god," Sebbie's face now had a permanent smile, accented by his wispy mustache, "Did you throw it out the window?"

"No, I—dude it's in my pocket!" Vel shouted, trying to dig it out while he drove and burning himself on the stump enough to yelp.

"*No way*," he laughed, "Nooo way! Why didn't you throw it out the window?!"

Vel winced and flicked it out said window, "And have it be there when we drove away? With *your* mom?"

Sebbie bent over to fish his CD book from under the seat, eagerly flipping through the pages of legitimate albums mixed with sharpie-written mixtapes. Even though he knew which page to flip to he still went one-by-one, looking over each familiar CD and handwritten song. "C'mon man, why were you smoking right before picking me up anyway?"

"I lit up to piss off my tía and didn't wanna waste it!" Vel protested, and Sebbie laughed again.

Finally he stopped at the back where *American Idiot* rested. It was Sebbie's copy, hastily given to Vel after his parents caught 'inappropriate' lyrics that made them fly into a disappointed lecture. Sebbie had narrowly avoided being grounded by protesting it was a radio station, slipping Vel the CD the next day at school for safekeeping. Soon Vel's favorite, safe-for-parents Owl City was swapped for Green Day.

"Awh come on!" Vel gave him fake shit, "My fireflies!"

Sebbie, eyes sparkling, flung it right back, "Seriously, Vel, who's the fag here?"

"I'm half-fag! Pretty sure, anyway."

"What *aren't* you half of?"

It took a second. But only a second, and then Vel grinned, glanced at his friend that was a foot shorter than him, and said, "Height, you halfling."

Another laugh and then Green Day filled the car. Sebbie

never settled back into his seat, animatedly singing in amateur harmonies with Vel. It was never clear if they tried to sing well and it didn't matter. Between the three of them slurs lost their thorns and became roses that stank of nicotine and chips. It was such a marked difference from the way he left his house. Solemn silence shucked off and Sebbie bloomed, energetic and fun and witty. Only when Vel drove Sebbie home did he retreat back into that protective shell, curling against the passenger seat of his car as he chose his favorite songs to play. Bright eyes closed, breathing far too steadily, too calm and distant. Vel had started counting the years with him to graduation, counting the years to where he and Dom would haul ass to get Sebbie out of that house. Dom had two gay uncles with connections elsewhere in the state, and if nothing else his mother was over-accommodating in her experience with caring for eight children. Dom being the last meant that she had only doubled her efforts before the nest became empty (or as empty as it would be with such a close family). Sebbie would be welcome.

"One more year, Sebbie," Vel said, and said to him often. This time it was returned with a gentle smile. One more year. It was doable. He reached over and skipped back to *Jesus of Suburbia*, voice cracking on the lyrics alongside Vel.

And there's nothing wrong with me
This is how I'm supposed to be
In a land of make believe
That don't believe in me

In the video store they hardly had eyes scrutinizing them as they trawled through whatever movies they desired, helped in no small part by Sebbie's hair loss standing next to Vel's towering height. Crusty B-movies, unrated and sun-faded for their irrelevance, piled in their arms—enough to last through dinner and well into the night. Once Sebbie eagerly paid for their rentals, it was off to Dom's house where if the pizza wasn't already ordered it'd be so shortly.

There Vel spread his long limbs out over the couch and ottoman in Dom's family room, squeezed comfortably between his best friends. Dom lamented the terrible writing and kept trying to fix it, Sebbie enthused over the effects both clever and bad, and Vel mimicked and mocked the acting from where many new in-jokes were born. Over pizza and soda and chips and salsa and candy and homemade cookies and whatever else the night passed on into morning. No other place that Vel preferred to be, no other place where he let his long limbs be comfortably unfurled, and no replacement for his time well spent.

It was Dom's turn to take Sebbie home, so at 6AM on three hours of sleep Vel hoarsely parted ways and drove home alone to crash in his own bed instead of pretzeled on a couch that barely had enough room.

Crash he did, falling into a deep and pleasantly dreamless sleep. It had become the norm for his Saturdays, where nothing could wake him until mid-afternoon. Usually he woke on his own, but that day, that fucking day, his tía knocked on his door. At first it was quiet to coax him awake, then when he didn't respond it was sharper, sharper, sharper until finally he gave in and groaned loud enough for her to hear.

The door opened, but instead of the bombastic entrance he was expecting along with a list of chores he missed, his tía cautiously poked her head in with the phone pressed to her collar.

"Jeró, get up. It's for you. It's Dom's mamá."

Vel scrunched his face in confusion and pushed his leaden body upwards, still in yesterday's clothes. As he reached for the phone he met his tía's brown eyes, careful and serious. That was odd. Bad-odd, and worse that it was Dom's mother and not Dom himself calling. Before she handed over the phone, however, she hissed a whisper at him.

"What did you do last night? Were you with them?"

"Wha, *huh?*" Vel furrowed his brow in confusion, "Just give me the phone!"

Staring at him, she reluctantly did. Dom's mother usually had a warm and welcoming voice paired with a calculating efficiency to balance eight young lives alongside her own. He had never known her to shiver or shy away from anything, but on the phone her voice was harrowed and afraid and, dare he say it, *small.*

Vel looked at his tía in shock. Then horror. Dom and Sebbie had been arrested that morning on suspicion of murder.

4

Hearing Dom's mother start to cry on the other end made anger wash over him. It was bullshit. It was *bullshit*, that's what it was. She knew it had to be a lie too, but what could she do? What could *he* do?

He hung up the phone and pushed his tía out of his room. He could prove their innocence, that's what. No, Vel *would* prove their innocence, even if it killed him. To do that, he needed histía to be totally oblivious. Changing clothes was a good excuse to shoo her away, and shirtless with his pants hanging open he dropped to his knees and reached under his bed.

Out came the first shoebox full of playboys and crusty socks, the shielding barrier between his tía and what was, in fact, more important: the second shoebox. Wrapped in his baby blanket and tucked so far back his tía would need a broom handle to fish it out. Unwrapping the bright pink and green colors revealed what he managed to salvage from his mother.

A wreathed effigy made of willow branches and an animal's spine. A case containing the eyes she had clawed out of her head in her final moments of life to give to him. Other odd trinkets and ends, including a leather cord necklace fixed with quail feathers and a rodent skull. Witchy things. *Useful* things. Vel bit his lip. He hoped so anyway. Anything he pulled out he'd have to be prepared to lose, and in truth he wasn't prepared to lose *anything*. But losing his friends to unlawful imprisonment was more pressing. It was still preventable. Deciding upon the necklace, he placed it on his bed before redoing the shoebox's defenses.

Vel blew past his tía, gruffly saying he'd be going out and didn't know when he'd be back. First she protested in English, but as it became clear he wasn't stopping she sped up until her words tripped into Spanish. Vel, frown etched onto his face, tightened his shoe laces and left before she could question the necklace bundled in his hand. No chanclas thrown at his car this time.

It was just on suspicion, right? They couldn't hold them forever without solid evidence, right? Vel's heart pounded as his teeth ground. His previous rage was simmering into a fine anxiety. Even though graduation loomed he had always seen it as the reins of freedom—especially where Sebbie was concerned. It never meant that he'd be losing his friends, only that they'd be more free to express their friendship. *This*, however, this, no. *No*. Who would be in their place if he lost them? Not even his Tía Gloria was his mother. They may have been sisters, she may have been his guardian in both legality and concern for his wellbeing, but no one on earth could ever call themselves his mother ever again. Losing the only true parent he had ever had left him numb and alone, staring blankly as his things moved from one bedroom to the next. The only feeling was the panic when Tía Gloria started throwing every semblance of his mother away—leading to Vel scrambling through the garbage can to salvage what he could. So who was he sitting between in the back of the classroom when his head was down, fraught with bloodied nightmares and digging his nails too deep into his skin?

Sebbie had been the one to break the ice, pushing a folded piece of paper against his lanky arm. It was a drawing of a jackrabbit, which at first clogged Vel's throat in terror. His mother had such an affinity for jackrabbits. How could this short kid next to him have known? Vel had brushed it off, even though he kept the drawing. The next day another drawing was slid onto his desk, this one of a dragon. It became clear then that Sebbie hadn't *known*, and was simply trying to cheer him up despite having never talked to him before. Vel melted, tears springing to his eyes that washed him in hot shame for being so vulnerable so publicly.

It hadn't mattered to Sebbie, though, nor Dom on the other side of him. The three of them started gravitating towards each other at lunch, and the rest, well. The rest fell into place like they had been friends since birth.

Five minutes later Vel had to pull over because he didn't know where the closest police station was and his cloud of thoughts certainly wasn't getting him anywhere. He looked at the hollow eyes of the rat skull at the center of the necklace, as hollowed as his mother's had been when he had found her. So, Mom? He was gonna get them out. Believing in that meant he'd find a way to do so, right?

Gingerly he laid the necklace around his head, wrapping it once over so it wouldn't bounce against his stomach or get tangled. Immediately self-conscious, he grabbed the rearview mirror and bent it to get a proper look at himself. It looked... Dude, *why* did he decide to wear the purple Charles Barkley shirt?! It looked so stupid and out-of-place underneath the witchy necklace. The rat's eyeless sockets stared at him through the mirror, scrutinizing.

Fuck, it didn't matter, Dom and Sebbie *needed* him. The necklace would surely give him mystic credibility. Vel sucked in a breath and kicked out his car door to ask for directions.

After five layers of embarrassment and just as many more minutes of arguing, Vel finally got his answer, buying an updated map of Tucson for the clerk's trouble. The second he got back into his car he yelled into the steering wheel from the hot wash of anxiety, swallowed it, and set off again.

He yelled three more times in the car. All of the anxiety had to be gone by the time he reached the station, and his car was a faithful enough companion to safekeep it. Vel flicked the rosary hanging from the rearview mirror when he arrived, watched it swing back and forth, then stepped out.

One breath sucked in. Two. Long before high school he had adopted his posture to fit the pecking order of the halls—slouched, scrunched, and unnoticeable. Even after puberty where he was pushing towards six-five he hung his head down and slouched his shoulders. Of course he told himself it was just so he could see where he was going, towering over near every other student there, even Dom. That may have saved him there, but the police station was a different matter. Vel straightened his back and raised his chin. The necklace slid against his chest in response to his movement and he winced, losing the posture and falling back to his default. With the rat's teeth resting gently on Barkley's head the necklace looked loony! Scrunching his eyes shut, Vel sucked his breath in again. Again. There was no way in hell he was walking into the station without something from his mother by his side, no matter how corny. He had to *own it*, which was far easier said than done. He re-straightened his posture, swallowed hard, tried to imagine it'd just be his tía on the other side, and walked into the station.

In high school at least he was in a familiar element. The police station, however, was a whole different universe. Vel froze, met with a fairly normal reception desk that sat in front of a fairly solid wall. Nothing notable. Nothing special—not really anything at all that could indicate this *was* a police station beyond the fact that the rest of the building was thoroughly blocked off. But that could be said about many other things; doctor's offices, dentists, larger companies with reception areas. No cop dragged in a delinquent past the threshold like an establishing shot of a TV episode. It was rather quiet, and that made his preparation falter.

His voice betrayed him when he spoke, cracking so clearly that his height wouldn't hide how much of a kid he was. A frantic glance down and that crack became a stammer. Bright purple Barkley shirt, cargo shorts, and twin knee braces? Oh, he wasn't fooling *anyone.* Still, he managed to relay that he was there for Dominic Torres and Sebastien Moore. The receptionist raised an eyebrow, and soon he was caught in a confused back and forth until it was settled that he was there to make a statement on them as individuals. Sure, he could work with that. Vel slumped in one of the lobby chairs and waited.

Before long his leg started to bounce anxiously. It wasn't like the sound in the lobby was muffled, but there was a distinct notion that just beyond the walls there was commotion he wasn't privy to. How far back did that commotion steep? How bad was it? It was mid-morning on a Saturday, surely any Friday night parties would be well and away cleared up. He released a breath of air that puffed out his cheeks, hoping he looked natural but well aware that he didn't.

A door to the back unlatched and Vel swung his head to the noise, watching in anticipation. Whatever or whoever he was expecting, Robocop or David Caruso, that was not who walked through the door. She was—well, she was probably average height. She was both short and yet the tight swagger with which she held herself was rigid enough to be towering. Vel decided to help that theory by slumping further in the chair, not out of intimidation but curiosity as she approached him. Her dirty blonde hair was pulled back so tight her scalp seemed yanked, and her gray eyes were hyper-focused without leniency. At first Vel would've called her stocky, but upon further reflection the boxy way she held herself simply upheld her strength and— yeah, she was uptight. No other possible interpretation. When she was close enough for him to read her name tag his mind scrambled on its collection of letters he couldn't parse—*A. Kulasiewicz*.

"Are you Mr. Jerónimo Velasquez?" she asked, her lips not breaking her frown. He'd like to say it was disapproval or belittling, but judging by the faintly forming lines on her cheeks it looked like her mouth was just *like* that. On purpose, no doubt, but still just *like* that.

"Sure am, uh, yes. Yeah that's me," he answered, shoulders to his eyes and hips out like a precarious bridge from the lobby chair. She did not look impressed, though it was unclear even to himself what he was trying to do, "Who're you?"

"Sergeant Kulasiewicz."

Vel strained, doing his best to untangle the sounds as they came, "Sergeant *Cool-uh-say...wick-z?* Right?"

"Kulasiewicz." she replied without a hint of emotion, neither grateful nor exasperated, "You'd like to make a statement on the two young men, Dominic Torres and Sebastien Moore?"

Two young men. Why did that sound wrong? Vel swallowed, "Actually uh, I mean yes, but also I was gonna offer my help."

She raised an eyebrow, "Help?"

Vel shrugged, trying to seem nonchalant and confident, "Yeah I got a certain way of looking at things that might see something you missed."

"Is that so," she said slowly, "And what is that, Mr. Velasquez?"

"Well I wouldn't know until I see the crime scene," he responded, barelyswallowing a *duh* before it left his mouth but the look in the Sergeant's eyes told him she heard it anyway. Yet if he had just bluntly said he'd witch his way about things he'd get booted without a chance. The Sergeant scrutinized him for another moment before pulling a chair up and crossing her legs to rest a notebook against.

"Provide your statement on Dominic Torres."

Vel blinked, pulling himself up to sit properly in light of the fact that he was suddenly strapped for descriptors, "Whaddya wanna know?" he asked.

"Who are you to him, and what do you make of his demeanor especially before the occurrence of the suspected crime?"

That was easy. "Dom's my best friend since seventh grade. He's big but quiet and sweet and thoughtful. Y'know, writerly type. Good in English class."

The Sergeant didn't nod as she wrote, making it hard to tell she was done until she asked, "And Sebastien Moore?"

That was *also* easy, "He's also my best friend. Sebbie's energetic and fun and loud. Quick to laugh and fills up a room despite his small size. And like, draws *really* good and pays attention better than me an' Dom anyways—,"

"Interesting." the Sergeant interrupted. Vel stopped.

"What?"

She looked at him, gray eyes cold and piercing, "Is that what others describe Sebastien Moore as?"

Shit. Panic flooded him and mixed with indignant rage, an explosive combination as Vel jerked forward in his seat, agitated, "*Others?* Like who?! And why! The three of us get bullied to hell and back, but *especially* Sebbie! We're his guards, right? Can't shove me or Dom into a locker! Whatever they said to you they're a *liar*, his parents don't know *anything!*"

Her gray eyes sucked all of the sound out of the lobby as she stared at him, and Vel fumed, determined to win the staring contest. It was only when she glanced down at her notepad and started to scribble again that the realization that he may have said too much sank on his dumb head. Being bullied as a motive for crime? Check. Lying parents, or was it Vel who was lying? Check. Angry outburst when challenged on *one minor thing* that if he had thought for *ten more seconds* he would've realized how to navigate what was a clarifying question and not an accusation? Check, check, check, Vel dug his fingers into the armrests of the chair and hoped she didn't notice that he was now desperate to remain on the offensive to cover for the fact that he *really* shouldn't be. Vel swallowed.

"Um. Me and Dom—Dom and I, we drive him around because he'll get a car when he graduates. So uh, last night was one of our movie nights, it was my turn to pick Sebbie up and Dom's turn to take him home this morning. And that's what happened."

"So," the Sergeant filled in, "No discussion of this prior?"

"Why would there be?" Vel dug his fingers in more, "Why premeditate an uh, why even do it at all? Sebbie was expected home."

The Sergeant didn't say anything. Vel stared at her, but when she didn't acknowledge it he peered over to her notes. Easy to do with his height, not that he ever said as much to his teachers. There was nothing immediately telling; she had taken pretty self-explanatory, factual observations about his words and less so his demeanor. That was a welcome surprise if anything, but upon glancing at her again he should've figured she'd be as much. Seemed like the type to smile at a joke and call it laughing. No, that was giving her too much credit. Either way, the most unfun person in the world being a cop seemed about right to him.

"Thank you for your time, Mr. Velasquez. If you leave a phone number, we will keep you updated on their case if you wish."

"Their *case?* Wait c'mon, it's a misunderstanding at best!" Vel watched her stand up and put her notebook away, then sprang to his full height despite the friction of his knee braces, "*Wait*, for real, I can prove it!"

Unimpressed, the sergeant sighed, "By what means? You reportedly went straight home and were not there for what happened. Further, you are basing your assumptions on personal relationships rather than factual evidence."

"You're kidding yourself," Vel moved to hound her to the door, "As if best friendships aren't evidence!"

"Mr. Velasquez," she paused, unintimidated by his height, "What would you contribute to the investigation if allowed to do so?"

The question—challenge, rather—caged in on him, illuminating the lobby's two exits as directions at a crossroad. Answer wrong and he'd be kicked out for being a fool, and there were a million wrong answers that he could conjure and no right ones. Actually, he brushed his thumb underneath the teeth of the rat's skull, it was more how to weave an answer into one that took the road he wanted. Vel didn't think in the long term.

It was act now or leave Dom and Sebbie to rot in a cell.

He glanced around the lobby, then settled on her name tag, "Your...first name is Anna." he guessed—but it felt right. It was the most basic of instincts, following things that had *felt right* for reasons he couldn't explain. Didn't really feel like witchery, but if he started describing it as an instinctual voice that whispered answers to him in his mind he'd be burned at the stake faster than Joan of Arc could appear to him in a saintly vision. So it was probably witchery. Or the Lord. Whichever it wanted to be in that moment.

No expression change. He stammered, pulling on the necklace until the pins of the quail feathers scraped on his dumb purple Charles Barkley shirt. Frantically he tried to search for something else, having nothing to ground him but the necklace. Eventually, hopelessly, he found himself throwing out a prayer:If his mom was out there and hearing him, *give him a break*—a direction, *anything* to say to convince the sergeant.

All he got was the pins of the feathers poking into the cloth of his shirt and his distress magnified. That was it? That was *it?* Dinky little pin feathers of a common-ass game bird scraping his skin because he was yanking on them? That was nothing! That was nothing that was—

"Birds," he blurted, and the answer solidified and he took a shaky breath. The bird that came to mind was a male California quail first. Working quick, Vel pulled interpretation from the sprung image, "Your...husband likes birds. I think." Female quail then, "No, uh, you do." Both of them side by side, "Together?"

Vel looked at the Sergeant, helpless for any sort of reaction to tell him he was on the right track.

Nothing.

"A medium, are you?" she said emotionlessly.

Vel deflated, "No." It might've been an adjacent idea but it was the wrong term for it. He wasn't psychic. Just a little...sensitive, or rather *observant* of the magic that already existed in the world. There was nothing supernatural about it, and certainly nothing supernatural about *him*, elsewise he should've burned up at every Mass his tía dragged him to.

Raising a finger to tap her metallic name tag, Sergeant Kulasiewicz spared no sympathy as she debunked him, "Anna is an easy name to guess from just knowing the letter A. Common enough, Polish enough if you take that into consideration. And," she turned that hand to him and spread out her fingers. He noticed it was the left, and further noticed a thin tanline on the ring finger, "Evidence of a marriage. Impressive cold read. Now go home."

"No," he said firstly because he couldn't figure how to tell her *how* he had come up with his guesses, secondly because this was not the road he had wanted to go down, "*No*, I'm serious, I can help, I can prove them innocent!"

"Mr. Velasquez," she warned, "Go home quietly."

"*No!*" Vel shouted, "At least let me talk to them! I'm not fucking leaving until you do!"

Her eyes narrowed, "Velasquez. Go home."

"Go home and do *what*? Nothing? Fuck that! *Fuck that*, I'm fucking—I'll find where it happened and go investigate *myself!*"

At that her stance became readied and low, "You will not."

"Screw you, man!" Vel started for the door but Sergeant Kulasiewicz braced her shoulder as a blockade. He snarled, using his long limbs to circumvent her. Shouting that wasn't his own rang in the lobby, likely from her to the receptionists to behind the door he had previously wanted to get through.

"Mr. Velasquez, we *can* and *will* detain you for 48 hours if it means keeping you *out* of our investigation." she warned, shouldering him back again.

Vel cackled. Make him miss Mass just like that? Perish (parish?) the thought. Tía Gloria would blast a hole in the jail wall and drive every officer to Mass right alongside him if that happened. Determined and on the verge of seeing red, Vel started to fight the sergeant just as dirty as he fought the bullies off in the school hall—violent but never so overtly so that he couldn't cry and weep that it was just his big dumb body that he couldn't control. His elbow grazed her ear a little harder than it had to, he tightened his wiry limbs and scrabbled over her legs, leaving dirt streaks on her calves as he broke free into a sprint to the door.

The awkward angle that he had started from—half-tangled with the sergeant—tweaked his knees in a way that made them scream and he went splat on the lobby floor. The shock of concrete sent stars to his eyes. The adrenaline in his blood wasn't quick enough to pick him up before the sergeant pinned him, flanked by two of her colleagues. Vel howled, scraping wildly and helplessly to where he saw his car parked just outside the lobby doors.

Cold cuffs snapped on his wrists and before long his lanky body was pulled back, back, back behind the other door. It was a blur, a blur of swearing and anger and his things getting confiscated and then the slamming lock of his jail cell.

Locked up, but more accurately locked *away*. What was worse was that there was no sign of Dom and Sebbie in any holding cells near him. It was just him, alone, with only the clothes on his back and no necklace to guide him.

5

Vel stepped away from the bars, fuming. Now fucking what, you idiot? A jailbreak? Sure! Like that was going to help, even—or *especially*—if it was successful. Put an *actual* APB on his head, yes officer, just go for the tallest brown motherfucker this side of the Phoenix Suns!

Besides. He couldn't abandon her necklace.

Vel puffed out his cheeks and let the air out, looking around the cell. Inspiration for the jailbreak whispered at every corner but he desperately tried to ignore it. Chipped green paint revealed the underlying layers of color on the bars, all some sort of painfully neutral tone. At about the height someone would place their hands the paint was chipped away so bad that the iron beneath was not only visible but rubbed silver-smooth, the jagged layers of paint framing the phantom fingers. The solid walls were the same sort of brick as his school. Vel smirked wryly at the elementary metaphor to be made and tucked that tidbit away for whatever future English assignment could use it. The clinging plumbing was stainless steel but still used enough that he could tell that it had seen and, how to put it, *tasted* much over its years of use. The smirk became a frown and he paced around the cell. For what that was worth. Without the bed on one side he figured he could at least try to stretch himself out to his full height, good for his knee stretches. But he couldn't exactly do much else.

Fuck! For a half-second he envisioned splitting his knuckles on the wall in frustration, a quick *pop* and they'd splay flat and bloody. But that'd do him just as much good as a jailbreak, wouldn't it? What a danger to himself, must be a danger to others, and on and on and *still* Dom and Sebbie were in jail and he couldn't do *shit* about it!

The shitcan was in the corner. Given that everything was so harsh and concrete, every sound would echo. Swallowing down what should've been embarrassment, Vel channeled his frustrations into taking a long, loud piss right into the center of the bowl for maximum effect.

No one responded. He felt both proud as though he had silenced them and angry as though he deserved a response. A brusque *"Shut the fuck up!"* so he could say *"No!"* He'd revel in that. Instead he got to revel at a stark nothing, the silence of a jail mysteriously empty save for him. Vel was so angry but forced himself to deal with it.

As time went on, though, that anger started to wilt. An hour alone with no window nor person to yell at started to push the magnitude of what being in the holding cell *really* meant. Would it go on his personal record? Could he scrub it away? How did he make a plea deal—actually, did he even know what a plea deal was? Was this the only holding cell block in this station? Where were Sebbie and Dom? Did they place him here specifically because they *weren't* here too?

And—his necklace...please, *please* let the officers treat that with dignity. In his experience the average person recoiled at dead things. Bird feathers were the easiest to digest, but in the worst way. Lots of people got *too* excited about that, talking about all the feathers they had found (or, "found") while walking about, and Vel didn't know how to internalize how commodified feathers were nor why that felt wrong. Skulls were cooler, but bordering on creepy. Other bones? Forget it. Something so unique and handmade as that necklace could be the point of curiosity or ridicule, and from an officer confiscating his stuff, well. The way the sergeant had called him *medium* set unease in his mind. Moments before he had been desperately praying for his mother to help him in any way, now he was wishing he hadn't brought herwith at all.

Vel closed his eyes and tried to force himself to breathe. Breath was as important as water. His mother had told him that while she watched him poke around a muddy creek. Flow brought *newness*. The creek he was playing in would not be the same creek tomorrow, nor would it be the same a mere five minutes later. So, he breathed, then looked at his cell again.

The bars caught his attention again and much for the sake of his sanity, kept it. He counted the layers of paint that he could see from the chippings. Four, maybe five layers. Perhaps there was a fresh coat every ten years or so. Fifty years of age—fifty years of hands wearing away the paint to the iron beneath. Vel picked at the edges, peeling away a sizable fleck of green. He thumbed it thoughtfully, then carefully wrapped it in sheer toilet paper before pocketing it. Jailbreak was no longer on his mind, but he figured that keeping a piece of those fifty years would amount to something. If nothing else, it was bleakly reassuring.

The hall door opened and he looked up, listening first with curiosity then dread as he recognized the cadence of footsteps.

"Jeró!! ¿Jeró qué hiciste? ¿Oye, qué tienes? ¿En *nombre* de dios porqué fuiste detenido? ¡Pobre mi *niño*! ¡Pobre mi *muchaho!* ¿En qué pensabas?"

"Oh, shit," Vel muttered, watching his tía waddle into view.

"You were gone for *three hours*, ¡¿y esto es lo que haces?! You will give me a heart attack y me muero. *¡¿Quiéres eso?!*"

"What was I supposed to do? Leave Dom and Sebbie to rot?!" Vel protested, hating that he was getting the gist of what she was saying without truly understanding it.

"Well, you are doing a good job of that!" she huffed, "Come, I'm taking you home."

Vel crossed his arms defiantly, "No."

Her hurried yet relieved mood snapped and she enunciated on a lower, flatter pitch, "No?"

"That's right. No." he narrowed his eyes. The guard that had guided her to his cell made the wise decision to not say anything, and in the gap between words everyone could've heard a pin drop. Well. Maybe not Tía Gloria. She focused on nothing but Vel, evidenced by the hardening of her features.

"No. No? ¿Me dices eso?¿No?¿Prefieres perder tiempo *aquí?* You're trying to get out of Mass again, and it won't work."

"Oh yeah?" Vel shrugged, "Mass ain't got shit to do with it. I'm staying."

Her face darkened with fury and she flew into a louder, harsher rage, Spanish blending into a rhapsody of noises that he couldn't and didn't need to parse. He just stood as she raged, pushing his tongue into his cheek while he waited.

"Also Tía?" he said when she inhaled, and she paused to hear him spew: "Fuck."

The bomb dropped and she exploded, this time with strings of English to *ensure* he knew what she was saying. Fine, she had concluded, he could *stay* there and rot with the criminals, see if she ever invited him home again, no candles lit, she was going and he was going to find his own way back. Nevermind that he had driven there in the first place, that wasn't important. Fury clouded her eyes, and she stormed away with equally colorful words to the guard that had brought her to him.

The guard blinked, flabbergasted for a moment. Vel, resting his arms through the bars, shrugged.

"She used to be a nun."

The guard laughed, "Used to be?"

"Yeah. My bad, I guess."

Another laugh as the guard shook his head and followed his tía out from the row of cells. Subsequently, Vel was alone again. And subsequently, he didn't know if he regretted how he had talked to his tía. Likely what the sergeant threatened had initially been empty, locking him up like a toddler in a baby pen until his guardian came for him. Rejecting that put more work in their hands. He sighed and sank into the flimsy cot. No one to blame but himself.

He dozed. They fed him. He dozed again for longer. It was never a full sleep: uncomfortable nightmares of his friends put up against the wall plagued him. He was cursed to watch, throat soundless as he screamed. Tía Gloria was there at his arm, trying to pull him away to spare him the sight of it. At the very least she never succeeded.

The sound of the door woke him and he blithely wondered if he was going to finally get a neighbor, but, no. The sergeant from before plus the guard appeared empty-handed. Vel sat up.

"Hey, thanks for helping me skip Mass," he greeted with a grunt, "Now can I go?"

The sergeant sighed, already sick of his shit. The guard smirked and tapped the bars.

"Still feisty today, huh? Didn't learn anything?"

"Oh. I learned my school has these same walls," Vel rapped his knuckles against the bricks in the same rhythm as the guard's, "You gonna help me skip Monday too?"

He chuckled, "What's next, basketball practice?"

Vel went deadpan, "I don't play basketball."

"What's the shirt for, then?"

"Wearing."

The guard scoffed. Hard to tell if he found humor in that. The sergeant predictably didn't.

"Kid, just be thankful you got a lucky break," the guard said.

Vel raised his eyebrows, "Huh?"

"You offered assistance in the investigation. Instead of holding you for another 24 hours, you may do so," the sergeant said, yup, humorlessly, "Under our supervision."

Whoa. After a day in the tank Vel had come to understand that his initial request was brazen and immature, acting like this was the movies. He stood up, winced because he forgot his knee stretches last night, and tried to hide it to look capable.

"That's, uh," he stammered.

"Provided you can get your ass in gear," the guard grunted.

"I mean. Put me in, coach? That's what they say on the court, right?"

"Got a little joker on your hands, K," the guard commented.

"Ain't little," Vel interjected.

"Unfortunately." the sergeant replied to the guard before dismissing him. She remained quiet until the door shut. True to his interjection, Vel towered over her like he towered over most everyone these days yet her gray-eyed stare put him on edge.

After too long a while, she spoke, "You said my husband and

I like birds."

Vel swallowed and nodded.

"Which ones?"

He thought. His first instinct was to ask for his necklace back but that risked charlatan levels of macguffin-ry. Pushing his tongue into his cheek, Vel thought, and thought, and thought. Back again to his mother, and water. Water had memory. And more than half of the body was water. All he needed to do was magnify it.

"Can I uh, have one of your hairs?"

She raised an eyebrow, "What?"

He gestured to her head lamely, "Just one. Not as a souvenir, I just need it to answer your question." Vel looked at her, "S'why I need to see the scene first before I can tell you anything." As if that explained it.

Scrutinizing him, she reached up to her hairline.

"A longer one, please, long enough to make a loop."

Her eyebrow perked up higher, but she did as requested and plucked a long dirty blonde hair. Vel held out his hand and wound a simple loop from the strand.

"Okay, now spit in my other hand."

"*What?*" her scrutinizing edge dug in but Vel jutted out his chin in defiance.

"Do you want me to answer the question or not? C'mon, put 'er there!"

Her lips teetered on a sneer, if not outright disgust. For a brief moment that was as exhilarating as it was terrifying. Vel thought she might turn on her heel and march away, leaving him to rot for another day before releasing him to the reality that he had managed to do nothing for anyone. Her gray glare dropped to his open palm and he fought the inkling to pull it back. Then, reluctantly, she folded her lips inward, pursed them, then spit.

"Dude, gross," he chastised, retreating both hands back into the cell, "Don't tell me you can't hock a bigger loogie than that."

That seemed to spark her distrust but she kept quiet. Vel counted that as a win. Relishing in it by pretending to ignore her reaction, he stirred the puddle of spit in his palm until it was sufficiently sized. Then he dipped the loop of hair into the puddle, creating a tiny lens. Wary of its fragility, Vel cautiously raised it to the light. Within the lens the vague shape of a bird began to form and he took in a breath, squinting to force the rest of the world to recede as he focused.

"Oh!" he said when the picture became clear, "I have no idea what this bird is."

"Describe it." the sergeant demanded, startling Vel.

"It's, uh," shit, how would Sebbie describe it? How would Dom? "It's gray and round, has a crest like a roadrunner but it's not that, I dunno, I've never seen it before."

"And its beak?"

"Huh?" Vel glanced at the lens again, "Yeah it's got one, it's a bird."

The sergeant stared at him. Vel did his best to stare back like he wasn't fumbling for a better answer, as if he even knew what a better answer would sound like. Then she blinked, pulling a notepad from her pocket and intently reading something she didn't share with him. She retained her stern expression but it seemed her contemplation had turned.

"You claim you can see things we may have missed?"

He perked up, heart racing for a good reason for once, "Yup. Real evidence stuff."

She looked skeptical, but then with a sigh that betrayed that she had little choice in the matter she closed the notepad.

"Alright. You may...*investigate.* Under my supervision."

"*Yes!*" elated, Vel's voice cracked, he coughed, adjusted it, and tried to speak deeper than he had been before, " —*Eurgh,* yes, yeah. Put me in, coach. Sarge. I can call you Sarge, right?"

She glared at him, "No."

"Cool. Lead the way, Sarge."

6

Vel was acutely aware that he was pushing how much he was asking for. After gingerly retrieving his necklace and other things (though he was not allowed his cigarettes) from the guard, he asked Sarge to take him home so he could pile useful junk into his backpack. Tía Gloria was still at Church, and so it was a relatively smooth in-and-out. Granted, he hadn't stopped to change his clothes, didn't even think to, even though he grabbed a baja hoodie he had borrowed from Dom and had yet to return. (It was big, it was comfy, and he may have smoked in it once and was waiting for the tobacco smell to fade—totally that, and not that he had forgotten.) The sergeant was less than pleased with her skewering stare, but tolerated it—both the backpack and the undeniable funky teen stench. Yeah, she definitely had little choice in this matter.

She ran him through the bare bones of the case. At about mid-morning on Saturday, a body was found crumpled on the side of the road near a park. The body had sustained severe blunt force trauma indicative of being run over by a car, and with the smear on the road nearby it was likely a hit and run. Sounded like baloney to Vel; there was no way Dom out of the three of them wouldn't stop, freak out, and call authorities if he accidentally hit someone.But he bit his lip while listening.

Before long they were tracing the route to Sebbie's house, not that Sarge knew anything about that. A knot started to form in his stomach with how stripped yet definitive the details were. Had the arraignment already happened? It was unlikely, unless someone wanted the case expedited. Were they searching for more evidence of the crime to convict—because if they were, they wouldn't be able to doanything. They were innocent, Vel wouldn't be moved from that. Innocent until proven guilty.

Unless...

There was an ill-conceived sort of joke to the way Sarge pulled the squad car up to the park. Behind her sunglasses he knew there was a bored glint about her; vaguely curious with what he was gonna do but overall expecting a tantrum at best and sheepish milling about at worst. Maybe the officers had placed their bets on what he would do before they left the station at all. Why weren't *they* collecting the evidence? Why send *him?*

"Alright. Find evidence." she grunted, effectively setting him loose. Vel hopped out, the knot in his stomach turning suspicious, and he glanced at her over his shoulder. She was already resting against the squad car with her arms crossed.

Why choose to give the sergeant the indignity to babysit him and not some beat officer? Vel tugged on his day-old smelly Charles Barkley shirt. Were the TPD sending a kid to do the investigation for them purely on the assumption that he'd fuck up and definitively send his friends to jail? Did he, did *they* really look like that much of a threat? Or was it just more convenient for them to close a case? He smushed a scowl into a wavered frown. Better not step out of line if he could handle it. Getting himself thrown in the tank was bad enough, but seizing this opportunity only to fuck it up was worse.

Vel scuffed the dirt with his sandal, then properly took in the scene. Sarge was parked perpendicular to the street he would take if he was driving Sebbie home. Fair to assume Dom took a similar route. He paused to motion to Sarge he was walking that way, then watched the ground as he traced his steps.

At the street corner Vel set his backpack down and pulled out a little toy car. Telling himself he'd definitely fix Dom's baja hoodie later, he wriggled a thread loose and snipped it, long enough to tie around the body of the car.

"...What are you doing?" Sarge asked and Vel yelped, sending the toy car careening into the air and clattering onto the sidewalk.

"*Jesus fuck,* Sarge! I was *concentrating*, that's what I was doing!"

Sarge didn't say anything, unimpressed and suspicious. Vel huffed and righted the car on the sidewalk parallel to the road.

"Look, I'm recreating the scene, alright?" he explained as though it was clear as day. In a way it was, but what was in his hands left a lot to be desired. Petulantly, Vel ignored Sarge's gaze as he meticulously adjusted the car's trajectory. Concentrating hard on memories of Dom driving his minivan (how he drove the speed limit and blamed it on the weight of the van, how his music ranged from Latin club beats to video game soundtracks) Vel rubbed some of his sweat on the front of the car and released it.

Without a push, it started to roll forward at about the speed limit. Vel stood up and jogged after it, water bottle in hand and leaving Sarge with his backpack. There was the an area taped off halfway down the block, about the size of a body, but the toy car didn't slow. Vel yelped and pumped his poor legs to catch up, splashing it with water to end the enchantment before it drove off into the sunset.

He doubled over, wincing though it had only been a short sprint. Sarge slowly approached, watching with intrigue but hell! For all she knew the toy car had a little motor in it. Exchanging a swig of water for himself, he looked at the dirt. Of course with a Saturday and an investigation already passed there were layers upon layers of footsteps, and with Sunday service about to be out it was gonna be trampled all over again.

"So," Vel nudged the car with his foot, "I recreated the scene. And the car didn't stop because it hit something or because it was trying to avoid hitting something. Or swerve. Or any of that."

Sarge sounded unimpressed, "Oh?"

"So like. How could Dom have run someone over? Even if he *did* hit someone there should've been a stutter, or a pause in speed or something."

"Yes." Sarge said, a full-stopped word. Okay Sarge. Sure. Make him yank it out.

"I mean," he started, frustrated, "If you assume innocence until proven guilty, then this would at best be uh, an accident, right?"

"Manslaughter." Sarge corrected.

"Whatever. You'd still need evidence that Dom *hit* anything, instead of trying to find evidence to the contrary. Right?"

"If you argue that," she shot back, "You will need hard proof. So find it."

Vel looked at her like she was crazy, "But—,"

"*Hard proof*, Velasquez." she paused, almost a full stop, then after a beat of consideration added, "Don't operate as though this is a misunderstanding. Enough time elapsed between the estimated time of death and the arrest that a car could be cleaned. You need proof beyond a reasonable doubt."

He wanted to bark back, throw that tantrum she was no doubt poised for him to resort to. But he bit his tongue. For a half-second he allowed his eyes to dart away, checking if he could see any disguised squad cars parked nearby—if not to harass him then to mock and jeer when he inevitably was a big kid about everything. Though he didn't see any it did not assuage his anxieties.

Hard proof. No tantrum. If they were using him to tank Dom and Sebbie's credibility, he better make it hurt them as much as they were gonna hurt his friends. Vel turned back to the playground.

"Hey, do you smoke?"

"No. And I'm not handing you a cigarette."

"Damn." Vel muttered, then wandered into the park proper. Start with the very basic of basics. He was headed towards a sun-bleached playground set, one he remembered in vivid colors when he was younger. Dotting the perimeters of the playground was the occasional bench for the parents to watch from, each one having a faded plaque with a faded name. To his right the park stretched out, mostly scuffed up grass for the odd spot of frisbee or soccer, with poles that suggested a volleyball net could be set up. In patches where the grass was sparsest, the dirt was kicked up into mounds by all the feet that used it. It was hardly abandoned but it had seen better days, or, no, Vel should reverse that. It had seen *newer* days, its wear now was simply proof of its use to the community. Although proof of that use was also proof of its familiarity, and by proxy he could guess how much it was taken for granted.

With the baking sun the scuffed grass was dry, yanked up by pounding feet and closed baby fists. Certainly not enough to pull memory from whatever water remained, leastways not within the time frame the sergeant implicitly gave him. The playground was not much better of a start. Where the sun didn't wear color away the many, many handprints did—not dissimilar to the jail cell but far less hauntingly so. Vel tapped the sturdy but hollow plastic, but couldn't pull anything distinct from the sound.

He glanced over to Sarge to glean any annoyance from her, if he was wasting too much time or if this babysitting gig was making her mad. It was hard to tell, especially with her sunglasses, but before he could awkwardly make chatter to fill in the void a roadrunner darted across the park. Normally it wouldn't have been noteworthy—until it tripped several paces in front of him. Vel watched in muted interest, wings fumbling and flapping as if the mound of dirt it should've seen popped up out of nowhere. Vel tilted his head. It was a mound of dirt, yes, but...as he approached it he realized it was not created by the regular scuffing of feet. Though its foundations were weakened, the dirt had been packed by small hands and covered with pieces of mulch from the playground. Vel crouched down and gently brushed the dirt away.

Curiosity turned to confusion, and he pulled a buried sucker from the ground. It was still wrapped and untouched as if it had been freshly pulled from a pack. It was also planted stick-down, and he wondered if a kid was playing pretend in growing trees. Or...whatever they were trying to grow. Burying a lollipop in the ground sounded like trying to homegrow a real-life Candyland to him.

He glanced up. The roadrunner was staring at him, and something about its intensity made him pause.

"Hey. This belong to you?" he offered the sucker. The road-runner's feathers puffed up and it squawked in indignation, a scraped-throat sort of tiny roar that would've made a dinosaur laugh, "No? Alright I'll just keep it then."

Beak clacks, loud and even more indignant, interrupted him and he raised his eyebrows.

"Well if you saw something, can you show me?"

At this the roadrunner preened its chest, not flinching even when Vel stood back up. Twirling the sucker between thumb and forefinger, he waited patiently until the bird was done and turned to keep on its original path. Vel followed, passing right by the sergeant.

"You comin', Sarge?"

"Coming *where?*" she asked, but her emotion was ruffled enough that it emboldened him.

"I find it's best not to ask directly," Vel said without looking back, "Presuming shit is the same as putting blinders on."

"Following a roadrunner is presumptuous enough," she huffed, and at that Vel glanced over his shoulder to meet her eye.

"You tell me, birdwatcher. Was that normal roadrunner behavior?"

Sarge was quiet, and Vel felt pride push a smile up his cheeks as he stepped onto the road the bird was crossing. Behind him he heard Sarge follow.

The road was solid beneath his feet, and remained to *be* solid. Stepping up onto the opposite curb, however, pushed the rest of the solid world away. Shapes shifted in the sun, not unlike mirages. Wherever he placed his foot down was the most stable shape, and every time he focused he found that his foot was on a different street, a different sidewalk, a different yard. The roadrunner continued in a straight line, unbothered by the shifting planes between its steps.

Sarge, however, was plainly bothered. Vel could hear her breath steal itself away in confusion, slowly mounting into quiet terror. Familiar landmarks would pass into focus, a street name, a storefront, a well-known blue palo verde, but nothing about it was comforting. The street name was ten blocks down when they couldn't have walked more than two, the storefront in a different direction, the blue palo verde in a different district. At one point she stumbled and he paused just enough to catch her elbow, keeping her moving otherwise she'd step out of pace.

"What—the *hell* is this?"

"I've heard that roadrunners bring good luck," Vel mused, comfortable now that he was in his element and the sergeant was way out of hers.

"*This* is luck? This is not luck." Sarge shot down despite the path her feet were taking. Vel shrugged.

"Eating shit in front of me probably wasn't very lucky, but I'll take what I can get."

"Did—you?" Sarge started and struggled to finish, "Did you do this?"

"What? No. The hell?"

"You *talked* to it."

Vel scrunched his face as if he was about to burst out laughing at the absurdity of it, "You can talk to it too, y'know. I didn't hear anything you didn't, I just made...I dunno, educated guesses."

Sarge was quiet for a long time after that, following as diligently as her stupefied state would allow her as the roadrunner navigated Tucson. There was only one more word uttered from her as they walked, and it was a distantly skeptical, "...Educated?"

Though it came off as very cool for him to not respond and

let his actions speak for themselves, in his head Vel knew that it was simply because he had no idea how to answer her. Was sensitivity passed down from his mother an education? It definitely felt like a skill to hone rather than something hereditary, or maybe it was hereditary in that it was a skill only she could teach how to hone. Magic was an ever-shifting borderland, visible only if he knew how to look for it in its limitless forms. Which, of course, meant that no one was truly an expert in magic even if they claimed to be, at least not holistically. His mother grew up in the Sonoran desert even if she had crossed the arbitrary border from the Mexican half to the American half. Her knowledge was honed to this area, and thus so was Vel's. He had never seen nor heard of a roadrunner tripping, so knowing that was not quite normal nor expected drew him to what had caused it to trip. It felt banal and silly, but he'd call it magic.

That magic led him, bewildered police sergeant in tow, to a quiet parking lot. The asphalt was sun-bleached, cracks filling in with orange dust blown in by the winds. Sparse grass stubbornly grew in those in-betweens. One side was bordered with hopseed bushes, giving it a closed-in feel with the building it was connected to. It looked like a small theater, once repurposed into a church, now wilting in disuse and waiting for the proper authorities to finally figure out what to do with its sad remains. Vel watched the roadrunner disappear into the hopseed, taking its shifting mirages with it.

"We're—," Sarge, now flustered, turned around in vaguely horrified wonder. Her BlackBerry fumbled in her hand as she pulled it out, clattering on the asphalt. Sarge didn't look down to pick it up, still turning her head around to try and parse what had happened, "This is halfway across town,"

"And in a quarter of the time too," Vel grinned, enjoying watching her squirm in what used to be sound logic.

"What...," Sarge breathed, "What did you *do*,"

"I *told* you, I didn't do anything," Vel protested, turning from her to start scouring the parking lot, "I just made an educated guess and followed it."

"Just like that?" she asked skeptically.

"Just like that."

"Then...," she trailed off, and though Vel's ear was perked to her his attention was being drawn elsewhere. Thank god, because he didn't exactly know if he could answer a person like her in any way that would be satisfying. Trailing to the mouth of the parking lot, Vel knelt down in front of a patch of dirt. It was loose for the most part, having not had enough cars driving over it to pack it down firmly.

"Hey Sarge, when did this place close down, d'ya know?"

With a solid, grounded question, a lot of her bewilderment shed and she replied, "Five years ago for sure, ten since the decline was noticeable I think."

"Uh-huh. You got a tape measure?"

"No."

He looked up at her like she was crazy, then looked around to realize he left his backpack at the park. Swearing, he stood back up with a strained howl from the pang in his knees.

"Okay. Well." He kicked up a sandal into his hands and squinted at the faded markings, "I wear a size 16. How much is that?"

"I don't know." she answered firmly, her lack of amusement having long grown into frustration.

"What kinda detective are you, anyway?" he jabbed, slapping the sandal back onto the asphalt to put his foot back in.

"Do *you* know how long that is?"

"What? No. I'm 17 years old." Vel played stupid, fully leaning into getting under the sergeant's skin now that she had no backup.

"It's *your* foot." she fumed.

Vel grinned at her, which darkened her glare. Then, loudly, he counted the steps between one tire track to a similar one about a car's length away.

"Uh," he stopped with his foot angled up into the air, "Less than five, maybe four and a half steps between these two tracks?"

Sarge, notepad in hand, wrote down the numbers despite herself.

"Feels like," Vel tried to imagine his car in steps, "A sedan?"

Sarge peered over, "The tires aren't wide enough for a truck."

"Does your fancy phone take pictures?" Vel asked, "The tracks look similar to me but you can like, CSI that shit, right?"

"I suggest," Sarge said, positioning the phone over the track, "that you stop watching TV."

"What are you, my tía?" Vel complained, pointing out other instances of the tire tracks along the dirt, "These all look the same."

Sarge nodded, then suddenly stopped. He was about to jeer at her for it when he recognized the dawning of a twisted scowl on her face. It was eerily similar to when his tía realized the depth of his maligning mischief. He then watched the effort she took to tamp the emotion back down, face returning to its cool, composed exterior. That. More than anything he wasn't used to someone so eerily composed, and it was deeply disconcerting to him.

"And what does all this have to do with anything?"

"Fucking hell, Sarge, do you know who the killer is at the start of CSI or not?" Vel said, turning away from the mouth of the parking lot to start scouring the rest.

"I don't watch TV."

"Sorry, let me translate. Fucking hell, Sarge, do you think Sherlock Holmes knew who the killer was at the start or not?"

"No, let *me* translate," Sarge snapped before he could revel in his cleverness, "Following a roadrunner into a parking lot has no clear bearing on the current case. Nor does taking measurements of tire prints. What does this have to do with a murder half the city away? For all you know, it could be a drug dealer here."

Vel suppressed a dismissive shrug and retorted, "Could also be a horny couple finding a quiet place to fuck," he glanced over at her to gauge her reaction at his bluntness, "I know these things too, Sarge."

That didn't phase her as much as Vel would've liked, and her voice turned punishing, "When I said *hard evidence*, I didn't mean *this*, I meant something *tangible*, something *tangibly related* to the case at hand, not these wild grasping at straws after some animal mysticism as if that has any bearing on—,"

"Hey Sarge," Vel interrupted in a non-combative tone, causing her to pause long enough for her to look at the discarded sucker wrapper he had found. Taking the other sucker out of his pocket he presented the two of them side by side, "Same brand, same flavor. What do you think?"

Sarge was quiet, and that quiet started to say more and more as time went on.

"It's a hell of a lot either way," he filled in for her, staring down at the discarded evidence in his hands. A wave of emotion suddenly hit him, a tide that his brazen anger and indignity had been keeping back. Carefully closing his hands over the suckers, he swallowed hard and didn't wince when his voice cracked this time.

"Can I see my friends now?"

7

It was surreal to find himself in situations he had seen on
TV over and over again. Though it was all similar it wasn't
the same enough. Maybe it was how *sensory* everything was;
the smoothed-over areas where hands had rested, the aged
yellowing of the plexiglass, the hairline cracks in the chair he
sat in—some of which had actual strands of hair stuck inside
from people he'd never meet. People that had sat between the
dividers to see incarcerated loved ones, and while he was there
as much the same, it was...different. Similar, but different. He
was already tearing at the seams between being an investigator
and a friend.

That seam ripped further when Vel saw Dom appear behind
the glass first. He looked pale in a way Vel wasn't used to. Dom's
family was Mexican enough with a palette across all shades;
one of his sisters was closer to Vel's complexion whereas
Dom himself was fairly light-skinned. Whether it was the
fluorescent lights of the room or the sleeplessness of his sunken
eyes, the paleness became haggard and ghastly. All things
considered he looked calm, even if his unshaven face meant his
wispy sideburns looked like unkempt muttonchops.

It tugged at Vel's heart.

It took a minute for Dom to orient himself correctly, even to the sound of Vel's voice. Perhaps even because of it. Vel was likely not a person he was expecting to see and the phone's quality was dogshit.

"You alright, man?" Vel asked quickly, knowing that no answer could really be truthful.

After a moment, Dom strained and settled on, "I'll be fine," Vel twisted his mouth, but before he could decide whether to comfort or be mad in his place he continued, "This isn't my mom's first rodeo with one of her kids tangling with the law. And with everyone else old enough to have jobs or careers, I'll be...fine. They'll complain, but I'm gonna be okay, I think."

Though tired, his quiet confidence held water. It left Vel a little dumbfounded on what to say next. Platitudes felt dry and ashen in his mouth. Beyond that he had no idea what Dom was looking for anyway, even if it was a relief to see each other. He had so little family compared to Dom; no siblings, no cousins, no sets of aunts and uncles that weren't committed to nunnery things even outside of the lifestyle. He strained to imagine all of Dom's siblings filing in one by one, driving in—hell, flying in if this went on long enough. Dom leaving the cell time and time again, to this very spot, to talk to them whether they were lecturing or supportive or just simply jovial to cheer him up. How could Vel fit in the spaces? Sure they were best friends, and that definitely meant something. It's not like Dom had to put up the same front with him that he did with his family.

Well, no, front was the wrong term, wasn't it? Dom had a different relationship with Vel like anyone had a different relationship with anyone. The fact that his masks could only be chalked up to simple teenagerhood and not any true contention with his family was as foreign to Vel as it must've been to Sebbie.

Sebbie, who must've seen Dom leave the cell time and time

again. If Sebbie left a cell to talk to his family it would've been... he could imagine that very, very, very well.

Vel sucked in a breath and felt a heavy darkness settle on his shoulders to muffle his voice. "And Sebbie?" he asked, "How's he doing?"

Dom blinked slowly as he caught the shift in tone, "You're gonna talk to him next, right?"

"Yeah, I think so," Vel assured, "I'll raise hell if I don't."

There was little relief in Dom despite Vel's adamant bluntness. He dropped his gaze to stare off into nothing and shook his head, "I...I don't know. He's been quiet. Like, worse than when he's with his mom quiet. I can't get a word out of him edgewise, and he's not eating much either. I don't know."

"Jesus," Vel swore, "Is it—have his parents been around?"

Dom stared at him. Then he inhaled, "No."

Though he'd like to say it was worse than he imagined, that was about par for the course. In the hours after school Vel recalled Sebbie swinging his much shorter legs when perched on the edge of the school gardens. Waiting for his mom to pick him up, rasping in his cracking voice to tell him how everything he wanted to talk about with his parents was silenced when they told him to talk about something else. No stories about games with his friends, that was too childish. Talk about books. No, not those kinds of books. So on and so forth, until Sebbie couldn't talk at all around them. He wasn't right enough. The more the sun lowered in the sky the more he folded inwards. Vel would watch as he kept folding inwards, and inwards, and inwards until his body was just a husk and his normally bright eyes stared out more catatonic than a marble statue. At least marble statues were crafted and maintained with love.

"I'll talk to him." Vel declared, blunter than before. Probably foolish too, but it felt right in his chest. Hot with anger, but for once not an explosive, uncontrollable, or confusing anger. This was laser-focused and bright, as much as Sebbie's eyes were. As much as they should've been.

"Is that gonna help?" Dom said, not out of doubt for Vel's determination but out of fear of the situation. Vel blinked, then realized he hadn't actually told Dom anything. Sitting up a little straighter he tipped his chin out and spoke with a firm tone—that cracked in his throat despite his desperate attempts to swallow the squeak before it got out.

"They put me on the investigation!" It was thrilling to admit out loud, even if he had his suspicions as to *why* they let a teenager like him poke around. Vel still expected some kind of awe, even the incredulous kind, but Dom stared at him with a pained sort of disbelief.

"You? What are you gonna be able to do?"

"Anything, really, and at this point *anything* helps." he answered with a huff. It wasn't a total lie, Vel did have a sense that he *could* do anything, and he wondered if the sergeant had half a mind to agree.The memory of her total befuddlement at the parking lot was one to revel in.

Now doing *anything* was both a blessing and a curse, because he had no wherewithal on how to narrow down all of the anythings into a coherent path to an answer. Unfortunately Dom seemed painfully *aware* of that as he stared him dead in the eye and said, "Vel, your character kicked the orc chief in the shins when you failed an investigation check and tried to pickpocket him, *and* you were trying to aim higher."

"That was a *dice roll*, Dom—,"

"*Then* you tried tying a bunch of chickens together to create a parachute to jump off a cliff when I had already labeled a few escape routes!"

"*You're* just mad it worked—and *exactly!* Who else would think to do that stuff?" It was his strength as a player and for all purposes it was his strength in this investigation. Maybe even his only strength to name.

Dom frowned, "That's...But that's a *story*, Vel. This is...,"

Vel shrugged, gesturing to their surroundings, "They threw me in a cell too, after making a big scene trying to see you guys. Got myself into all that trouble and they still thought I'd be able to help."

It's not that Dom didn't look convinced, it was more that there was not really a way out of the labyrinth without going through the labyrinth anyway. Still he sighed, and, taking that as resignation, Vel gave one last little push.

"And if I get you tried for life, y'can blame it on me and take me out later. Sound good?"

Dom snorted, "Sure. Sure, Vel. What do you need to know?"

All the details Dom gave of the drive home early Saturday morning seemed normal. The sunrise was peeking over the long horizon, the sky was that sweet bluish-green, and nothing ran out in front of his headlights—not even a lizard. It was uneventful, his music was soft, and Sebbie was curled up the way he always would against the passenger side window. Dom noted that Sebbie had mentioned not sleeping well and had taken the opportunity to catch up during the drive. There was little else to distract him. When he dropped him off at his house there was the usual light on and his mother was sternly waiting with a steaming mug of coffee in her hand. Sebbie slunk out and bade him good night. Good morning. Whatever it was, and he didn't laugh. That was painfully normal, as was the drive back home where Dom crashed before the cops knocked on his door some four hours later.

Before Vel could ask forfurther detail their time was up. He could barely thank Dom before he was pulled back behind the door. Left for a moment by himself in the booth, Vel absentmindedly kept the crackle of the receiver to his ear. Semi-hushed voices from other booths momentarily distracted him. Emotional pleas, gruff disinterest, viper-like anger and disbelief; all were present and yet not as present as he thought. There was a low hum in each voice speaking, whether the voice seemed to acknowledge it or not. The hum that connected them: That despite whatever happened they *came*, they were *here*, and they *all* held a phone receiver in their hand. Something in his gut jumped to call it love, but he hesitated. He didn't know why.At the same time it didn't feel like *love, strong*, but *love, quiet*. How to draw the distinction between the two he didn't know, and when the door opened again Sebbie slunk through, shoulders hunched and bald head gleaming in the harsh white light.

When he saw Vel sitting on the other side his spirit lifted his shoulders as his eyes grew wide and bright. As they always were to him, as they always should be.

"*Vel!!*" Sebbie mushed the filthy receiver to his face, over-joyed despite the pale wash over his features; the very same that Dom had.

"Hey dude," Vel said, happy to see him but restraining himself all the same, "You alright?"

"I'm alright—," he answered quickly but something twitched in his face and it fell, letting the platitude fall with it, "I'm...actually...,"

Vel shook his head to let him off the hook, "Room service is shit here, I know."

At that Sebbie's voice fell further, "They threw you in jail too?"

"Don't I look like a criminal?" Vel perched his brown chin in the space between his thumb and forefinger, cocky for the hell of it, "I'm here cashing in all my good boy points just in case they pull me over again."

Normally that would've gotten a loud, if quick, laugh from him, but Sebbie huffed so meekly it barely disturbed the wisps of his mustache. Vel hoped it wasn't obvious that he took notice.

"Yeah? How's that going?"

"They actually did throw me in a holding cell, yes." Vel said so plainly it should've been funny, but he could see mounting terror in Sebbie's expression.

"Vel...," he breathed, and Vel quickly put up a hand to placate him.

"Hey I got a sweet gig out of it, they put me on your guys' case. Cool, right?"

The absurdity and suddenness of what he said knocked Sebbie out of his anxious shutdown and he blinked, "Wait—*what?*"

"Hell yeah!" Vel said, then felt sheepish as if *hell* was going to get him in more trouble. When no one moved he shakily regained himself and continued, "Like, listen, at this point whatever helps, and if I can figure out stuff to help your case, all the better, right? I just talked to Dom, but give me your side."

Sebbie laughed, and though it was in total incredulity it made Vel smile just because he was able to make him do so, "Alright, so, uh, where do I start, detective?"

"*Oof*," Vel grunted, "Actually, 'detective' doesn't feel as good as I thought it would,"

"No?" Sebbie's smile remained on his face, "But it's something, right?"

"Guess so. For whatever it's worth. Neither of us are eighteen yet. Blip on the paper that'll go away, right?" It was such a bold lie, but it was also a dumb mercy they could cling to.

Sebbie, curled up into his own arms with the receiver pressed flat against his face, glanced up from his contorted position, "I don't know, Vel. Aren't you scared? Being in a place like this?"

He shrugged, "A little. I dunno, I'm more worried about you guys. Plus like, y'know. I was born barely legal. Kinda washes off a lot of the...I dunno. It's like the first time you get punched in the face versus the twentieth."

That sobered him a little and he nodded, still keeping the receiver pressed hard to his skin as though he could physically feel Vel's presence through it. After a while a tired, morose, but sincere crackle came through the phone as Sebbie muttered, "Thanks, Vel."

"Oh, for what?" Vel played sarcastic.

"Since no one else came to see me."

Gutted, Vel's smile dropped. He stared at his friend, now hollowed out, lost looking at the metal joinings where glass met table and picking aimlessly at one of the screws. Sebbie did *mean* his gratitude, but was so defeated that it hardly mattered. Fatty, Cripple Kid, and the Fag could only have so much grounding self-esteem as a group anyways.

Taking in a breath, Vel spoke low and soft in the hopes that it'd reach Sebbie wherever he had sunken into, "I still have those drawings you gave me back in middle school."

Sebbie glanced up.

"The dragon's on my wall. The jackrabbit is uh, I keep that with some of my mom's things."

Sebbie's breath fluttered as he perked up. There was a flush of incredulity as his mouth curled up just enough to expose his front teeth, "Really?"

Vel nodded, "It was her favorite animal, in a way. Y'know. Kept it close to her heart. That's why I might've uh, acted weird when you handed it to me first. 'Cause it almost meant *too* much. And...well...,"

He hesitated for a moment. He had once hinted, deep into one of their movie nights where they had turned the volume down because they were too tired to hear things anymore, that his mother had been accused of being a bruja. Saying that in the broad daylight would make it sound like a farce, but under the blanket of the early hours where nothing moved meant that Vel had been serious. Even with that, most people probably wouldn't think much of witchery. At best it was an archaic accusation and his friends wouldn't have believed it was as serious as it was. Reaching into a surge of courage, Vel pushed up against the boundary.

"I think she's helping. Not *her* specifically, but the magic she taught. The Witch stuff—really really. Y'know?"

Sebbie started to laugh again, but upon meeting Vel's eyes his smile dropped.

"Yeah really," Vel reiterated, "Like I'm using it and I think it's gonna get you out. For real."

Sebbie stared at him, silent but thinking and thinking deeply.Discerningly. Vel knew he was goofy but because of that his flaw was being too easy to read when he was serious. He saw confusion twitch at the corners of his friend's eyes, and the longer the silence dwelled the more something skittered in Vel's gut. Of course Vel had never clarified what kind of magic his mother was accused of, but from the way he spoke it was clearly very different from tacky crystals and tarot cards. It was enough to chase her out of a whole country. Since Sebbie could connect the dots, he must've figured that it might've gotten her killed, too. What witchery, then, justified murder on that level?

The skittering started to scratch at his stomach walls, reaching against the depths of his skin and suddenly Vel felt a wash of sweat break out. In the years after 9/11, his mother had stood closer to him in checkout lanes and store aisles. It had not taken him long to figure out that there were people staring at the copper color of his skin a little too long. Discerning who he was and what he was doing there. His mother, being of much much fairer skin to the point where he looked adopted, had shielded him from the worst by simply taking his hand firm. Saying, with just a gesture, that he belonged to her and not to whatever violent fantasies the quivering stares imposed.

But Sebbie was his best friend, and surely he would come to the right conclusion. That Vel hadn't *meant* anything by implying that magic was real, he just meant he could help. That he wasn't that different. He looked weird, he stuck out wherever he went, but he wasn't different—he was only as different as Dom was, as Sebbie was, that's why they were all together.

His mouth twitched. It couldn't be laughed off. Sebbie didn't say anything into the phone receiver, and Vel hoped that it was for his sake. As to what Sebbie was *actually* thinking, Vel could only guess and his anxiety was doing the guessing for him.

"Seb," Vel spoke carefully. But before Vel could ask more, their time was up and Sebbie was pulled away. He chanced a glance over his shoulder at Vel, retaining that same expression of deep discernment thought even as the door closed behind him. Vel's heart raced, both in fear and in something else. Fear, because he was suddenly frantically dissecting every conversation he had ever had with Sebbie, fear that Sebbie might pick up on the fact that Vel might be the same as his mother. That a Witch was real like the gruesome fairy tales they all grew up with and not the kitschy feel-good fantasy the term had been twisted into. That fear soon overtook any investigative thoughts, because in the end it all culminated into the threat of rejection.

Sarge interrupted his spiraling mess, fetching him with an emotionless demeanor that did not betray that she had just stumbled through the whimsical journey of following a bird across the city. She hardly cared to look at Vel when she spoke, guiding him into the cornered off cubicle that was her office.

"Alright, Velasquez. You want to be a detective for a day, you have to do detective duties."

"Huh?" Vel, shaken out of a dreamlike state, frowned, "I was gathering witness testimony."

Sarge, unfazed, said, "Yes. And now you have to file the day's paperwork."

Slapped, stunned, struck, punched, dumbfounded and stupid, Vel croaked, "Paper-*what?!*"

8

Not only had Sarge pulled him back to her element, there was an air of smugness to it when she pulled papers from the printer, explaining what each one was and how it had to be filled out. And *what* had to go onto it, meaning that Vel was suddenly tasked with the utter disaster of explaining his actions from the roadrunner to the parking lot. Though Sarge had to do much the same, it wasn't *her* absurd actions she had to explain.

Vel collapsed into a heap of limbs and despair. The weekend started out with shirking homework in favor of spending time with friends and it was ending with something *worse* than homework and his friends behind bars. How in the *world* was that fair? He eked out decent scores on English essays and stories, but only just barely and usually with Dom's help. That was the only skill that remotely helped him here; poor scores in math and poorer in science were working against him. It wasn't like he didn't *understand* the science! He just took...creative liberties with it, winding up with bad marks and harrowing lectures from his tía. If it was that bad in the school halls, he could just imagine how far that'd get him in a police station.

Struggling with how to explain things in a way the adults would accept made the time tick with little to no progress. Sarge made it look effortless, though just as with anything else it was hard to gauge if she got any real joy out of it. This was only notable because her lack of joy in other things led Vel to believe that she might've been the type to find joy in the mundane bore that paperwork was, but alas. She hadn't even seemed that perturbed after she had to call an officer over to give them a ride back to the park earlier, though that gave Vel the personal joy of watching her try to explain how they got across town without a car. That was probably half the paperwork she was filling out.

"It's not that difficult," Sarge said flatly after the second time she asked him what was taking him so long, "You simply relay the information as it happened."

"C'mon Sarge, do you even hear yourself? How are *you* saying what happened?"

She was quiet, her pen checking boxes before cross-referencing with her computer screen, "As it happened."

"So you're writing *I followed a teenager following a roadrunner across town and the only thing we got was a stupid sucker wrapper?*"

"Essentially." she said, and Vel released a sound like a deflating balloon, collapsing into the chair until his legs were sticking out much the same as when he first met her.

"But they're not gonna *believe* any of that," he complained.

Sarge graced him with a momentary glance and raised eyebrow, "Yet you were so confident earlier that this could all be done."

"I didn't know I'd have to *write it out!*" he wailed, pitching a piece of paperwork over his face to attempt to cover his exasperation.

"Aren't you magic?" she asked without flair, "Can't cast a spell to have it done?"

"It doesn't work like that," Vel countered, not realizing he was once again speaking with confidence. He didn't need to prove anything to Sarge and it didn't matter to him if she stuck around him in the long term. Paradoxically he didn't care what she did or didn't know, especially after the roadrunner, "Otherwise I'd do it on all my homework."

"How *does* it work?" she asked, and Vel peeked an eye out from beneath the paper.

"So you admit it *does* work?" he prodded, and the next glance at him was a warning, "So the bird was correct?"

"You never named it." she deflected simply.

"No, *you* never named it! What's it called? Round ball of gray with a crest and small black beak, right?"

"I'm not saying its name in front of you."

Inspiration struck Vel and he shot up in his seat, snatching the paper from his face, "Is it a tit? It's a tit? A round fluffy tit?"

That pulled Sarge from her job, bracing her head in her hands and sighing with thinned patience. A grin split his face and his voice got louder explicitly for her torment.

"It *is* a tit! You like tits! That's so—,"

"It's a *tufted titmouse*," she sourly corrected.

Vel howled with laughter.

"Enough—*enough*," Sarge tried to regain control. Though the station was sparsely populated this late on a Sunday, there were still heads popping over and around the cubicles to stare. Sarge, harshly ignoring it, pulled them back on track, "If magic works for some things and not others, why?"

Vel shrugged, "Guess it's just my bad? I only know a little bit."

"What are you doing when you're...what would you even call

it? Casting spells?"

"Like D&D?" Vel scrunched his nose, "No, not really. I mean, I don't know. I guess you could call it that. It's more like... intangibly believing in the pulse of everything, I guess. Quietly tapping on the door of whatever you're trying to reach and asking politely if they'll help."

Sarge scrutinized him while the wheels turned in her head. He shrugged again, hoping he was getting the point across that this was all just as hard to explain as it was to hear.

"So how did you know things that you shouldn't have known? Things beyond a cold reading?"

Another, bigger shrug, "I dunno. Hey Sarge do you have kids?"

She narrowed her eyes, "Do you think I have kids?"

Vel placed his palms on the edge of her desk to hoist himself up, craning his neck far enough to look at a picture frame near her computer monitor.

"Yeah—two. A boy and girl."

Sarge let out a breath of exasperation.

"Like I said, it's not a test-taker or a chore-doer or anything like that," he continued, "So I don't rely on it, don't wanna lose sight of the real world because I think that'd be losing sight of what makes magic tick anyway."

"The real world making magic tick?" Sarge asked.

He nodded, "Y'know in the cell? The holding cell? You asked me a question about yourself, so I needed a lens that magnified your memories. So if I built the frame from one of your hairs and fashioned the actual lens from the water in your body, then I'd get a little magnifier built from you. Like spying on bugs or something, getting a glimpse of something you wanted me to hone in on. Lenses and magnifying things with concave—

convex? I can never remember—stuff is real, tangible. All I did was put a little twist on it."

She processed for a long time before cautiously relaying her thoughts, "That...sounds like it makes sense. But it doesn't."

"There, you're getting it," Vel charitably allowed, "I'm flying by the seat of my friggin' pants making shit up as I go, and that's where the magic is."

"Didn't you just say there was some sort of magic in what— my hair? My saliva?"

"Well sure," Vel stretched out his legs with a groan, "It's a miracle we're here at all. Scientifically it's not impossible but it's still a rarity so much as we can figure it, right? Then just, being born. Like what if our parents didn't meet? Then there's everything else right—what if I fell from a tree and cracked my skull open when I was a kid? What if I just dropped out of high school? What if I didn't try to skip Mass every week? So there's magic in the fact that we're sitting right here shootin' the shit and not doing paperwork."

Sarge opened her mouth but Vel quickly snapped up the air before she could turn them back to work again.

"*And* there's magic in just. I don't know. Simple things. Love and friendship and all that shit. Why does one asshole say one thing and it sucks but when your friend says the exact same thing it's different? Funny, even? I don't know, man. A roadrunner tripped and it seemed weird, and there's nothing about magic that ain't weird."

He looked over to Sarge, expecting some sort of deep contemplation or some wondrous stare that he was such a well thought-out teenager, *but*...no. Not at all. Now, she wasn't*unimpressed*, which was an improvement, but there was an element of dread he didn't expect to see.

"What?" he asked, accusatory first as a front. Beneath that the same anxiety resurfaced: the gut reaction that he had said too much to the wrong person. Fleeing a country is one thing but fleeing a second is a whole other thing. Maybe it didn't matter to him if Sarge knew because she wasn't important on an emotional level, but on a *legal* one...Well, he hadn't thought that far ahead and hated that he didn't. Vel was about to swallow and fire back another witty shot when Sarge simply groaned.

"Do *not* major in philosophy."

"Oh *come on*," Vel wailed as relief shot through him, "You and my tía both trying to rig my life up!"

Sarge snorted, further giving him relief by the mere semblance of amusement, "What does she want you to major in?"

"Religious studies."

"Just as bad." Sarge muttered.

The phone rang. Sarge picked it up with the flattest enunciation of a name Vel could imagine, but not only did she seem like she was expecting a call she was *also* expecting who was on the other side of it. Someone sounded pissed off, and specifically pissed off at Sarge. Vel watched in astonishment as her face remained unflinchingly solid. His tía certainly wouldn't have remained so calm—in fact she would've been just as animated as the voice on the other end of the line. Especially since it was Sunday, which was exactly the voice's chief complaint. He should've been home drunk and watching M*A*S*H instead of stuck on whatever errand Sarge had requested of him. Sarge, meanwhile, was responding monosyllabically, dotting I's and crossing T's as she waited for the tirade to end with the information she needed. Then she hung up the phone and stood up.

"We're heading out."

"*We?*" Vel said, unable to hide his intrigue and excitement (especially at the prospect of leaving paperwork behind).

"To the medical examiner's office." Sarge replied.

Excitement crashed with horrifying reality, blending into opposition in his chest, "Oh. Oh boy."

* * *

The Pima County Medical Examiner's Office wasn't quite what Vel expected, albeit in the same way the police station surprised him. The front of the building felt obliquely mundane in a way that was unnerving: Violent and suspicious deaths were kept in its clean halls all behind a simple receptionist's desk.

Besidethat front desk was a short man with a hawkish nose and a mottled bald head, abrasively complaining to the receptionist as she nodded along. In his hand was a steaming cup of to-go coffee even though it was late enough in the afternoon to be early evening. By just looking at him Vel could tell this was the ornery voice on the phone, to say nothing of how he oozed assholery despite the professional lab coat he wore. At their approach he squinted at Sarge with piercing annoyance. Then he clocked Vel at her side and his face soured further.

"K, what the hell is this? Bring a kid to work day? What is he, a wannabe CSI agent that watches too much TV?"

*What a thing for a guy that'd rather be drunk watching M*A*S*H to say,* Vel wisely remarked in his head. Out loud, he cockily postured, "How do you know I'm a kid?"

"Oh, he's snotty too," he grumbled, "Where did you find him, in a grocery store parking lot?"

"He offered help on the investigation." Sarge explained plainly.

He coughed on a gulp of coffee, "That's rich. TPD recruiting younger and younger every year, huh?"

Sarge was quiet at the jab, and it seemed that it might've actually bothered her. It was not a slight that the medical examiner seemed to care about, keeping his glare steady.

Vel piped up before the silence turned truly awkward, "No seriously, I can rent whatever movie I want. How d'ya know I'm a kid?"

His full scrutiny turned to him. Without needing time to think he dressed Vel down, "You've got too much cheek fat right at the front of your face and too many bones. Not enough post-pubescent padding to fill your frame out," he glanced down which Vel was thankful for because he had self-consciously pushed his hands to his cheeks to test their pudginess, "Your knee braces are one-of-a-kind paired together. Body's ripping itself apart as we speak and you ain't done growing yet."

"I'm not?" Vel's voice cracked. *God damn it.*

"*Humph*," he sounded rather pleased with himself, "Also, you stink worse than a high school locker room."

Finally, Vel joined Sarge in stunned, awkward silence. Trying to be inconspicuous, he sniffed himself with a slight turn of the head. Well. Remaining in his unchanged clothes only amplified the filthy teen funk. Which, he *had* known it was there, but he was suddenly sheepish at the thought of just how strong it was. The medical examiner took a long, arrogant sip of his coffee.

"Bosman," Sarge finally addressed, "The body. Please."

He grunted, "Scarin' the tyke off, huh? Tired of babysitting? Well, I can agree with that."

"Scare me off?" Vel said, a growing darkness hiding in the base of his throat, "I've seen a dead body."

"The body's been hit by a car, kid," Bosman explained

unkindly, "Like a bunch of rectangles punched in, pulverizing bones and bruising skin if the tires don't rip it clean off. Do you know where the word '*mangled*' came from? Kids getting their hands stuck in old laundry machines and having their skin shorn clean off. Now think of that between a tire and the road."

"Alright," Vel said, growing annoyed in retaliation, "So what?"

Bosman sniffed derisively, "Put on your tough face all you want, you ain't seen anything like this before, and I don't carry those little airplane vomit bags so you're gonna have to run fast with those knee braces of yours."

Sarge was of no help in the onslaught, "He's right. This is your chance to leave."

That made the anger at the base of his throat bloom—that Bosman was right, this was just for her to get rid of him by harshly rubbing his face in reality. Like a dog. A goddamn dog, "I'm not leaving," he huffed, "You *brought* me here, anyway."

"Sure, sure," Bosman dismissed, "Just telling you it's not as pretty as a funeral."

Vel snapped and snapped quietly, his voice glowering and low, "I found my mother in the kitchen."

Both adults went quiet with their full attention. He wished it felt good.

"I think," he was horribly aware of the rapid expansion and deflation of his chest, "that if she had had a proper funeral it would've been closed casket anyway." No salvaging a face with the eyes brutally clawed out; eyes that he cradled in his prepubescent hands as they shone with her blood. Blood that was drying too fast, because he wanted to scoop it all up and pour it back into her body if he worked quick enough before it dried. It wouldn't have done anything. He knew it was illogical.

But it was what his panicked heart thought he could do, even as his knees pressed into the slick tile in defeat.

As he watched Bosman struggle to think of what to say, feeling the sergeant's wide eyes on him in the strongest expression of emotion he had seen from her yet, Vel declared checkmate with a small, swallowed, "I was twelve."

They were *finally* taking him seriously and it did not feel good. No doubt Sarge had gained invaluable insight as to why Vel was so stubborn about this. Whether or not that gave him a leg up or just paved his road with eggshells he couldn't tell.

Bosman took another sip of his coffee and said without looking at him, "Well, that'll either make it better or worse."

Despite everything else that was an answer Vel accepted. Still not looking at him, Bosman waved for them to follow down the hallway to the morgue proper. He paused in front of the doors that were dinged and dented from many gurneys over the years. Vel wondered then how long Bosman had been working as a medical examiner and what that really meant in a fairly populated area.

"Last chance, kid." he warned. Vel didn't budge. With a shrug, Bosman opened the doors and led them to where the body was stored. Vel took in a breath and held it. Maybe he should erase all perceptions that he was going to look at a human being, with hopes and thoughts and people that loved them. That was what Sarge and Bosman seemed to do, Sarge especially. Vel wanted to brashly believe they were wrong for doing so, because try as he might he was having trouble with the idea of stripping a body's inherent humanity. That went against the whole principle of why crimes were solved in the first place.

Even so something nagged at the back of his neck, something

that knew that their distance from the body was not so much a personal attack as it was personal protection. Vel was angry at that, angry that it had to be that way, and *angrier* still that in the end the dead body did not matter to him like Dom and Sebbie did. Sure, they were alive. People like his mother weren't. His mother was too dead and too undocumented to matter. Yet when Vel talked about her, everyone got quiet. Because she was important. She had to be.

None of this solved Vel's argument.

Bosman pulled the body out of the wall with a grunt. Vel blinked, watching as he gingerly peeled plastic away from malformed bulk. It was soon terrifyingly clear that the plastic was there to keep the parts mostly in order. He watched one of the arms flop to the body's side, attached but crushed. The skin was distorted and bruised, darker and darker in the wide valleys caused by the car tires. Vel bit the inside of his cheeks, glancing at the head as if that'd give him respite when it was clear by the skull cracked in front that it wouldn't. The body was male, with more details piling in from Sarge who started stating them in a manner colder than the fridge Bosman pulled the body from. His name was Maximilian Green, he was in his mid-forties, a botanist and gardener interested in local flora and conservation efforts. He was survived by his wife Rita and college-aged children. The nagging voice at the back of his neck definitively struck him with *why* it might've been beneficial to pull away from the humanity of it all. When he believed so firmly that his friends hadn't killed him and the first names he heard were the victim's surviving wife and adult children, well. It was too easy to start guessing, and Vel had to struggle not to create false leads where there may have been none because of the fumbling determination to keep his friends innocent.

Focus. *Breathe.* He was there for a reason, no matter how selfish.

Green's skin pushed inward with the firm shape of the tire that killed him. Vel used his height to lean over the body to peer down at the print, "Sarge, can you look at the pictures you took in the parking lot?"

"It's not a fingerprint, kid," Bosman tersely interrupted, "The same brands of tires put out the same treads on the mass market."

Vel glanced up, "But a minivan is not gonna have the same size tires as a sedan."

"Potentially." he grunted in turn.

Vel countered, "Potentially has room for potential." Sarge turned her phone to Vel and he squinted. It looked similar enough, but part of him was still banking that they had some sort of pattern recognition program to boot up, just like in the TV shows Bosman accused him of watching. Then again, if the medical examiner was funded like his school, they probably didn't have that even if it did exist.

Still, what interested him the most were the measurements. Vel hovered his hand over the tire print on Green's body, eyeballed the width, and popped his foot up to lay his hand against the sole of his sandal.

"We got measuring instruments." Bosman interrupted again. Vel's balance teetered and he set his foot back down.

"Sure, but Sarge didn't when we followed a roadrunner halfway across town to an abandoned parking lot with similar tire prints. If *not* the same, they're at least the same width."

Bosman looked at Sarge and barked, "*What.*"

"Don't look at me." Sarge deflected with a very *I can't explain it even if I wanted to* tone. A vitriolic back and forth began between them, Bosman questioning Sarge and Sarge giving curt answers that never built the full picture to try and dodge answering all together. While they were distracted, Vel took the opportunity to observe without callous interruption.

It was curious that the skull seemed to have the worst fracture at the forehead when the tire seemed to flatten his frontside. In his mind, if a car ran him over from the front it'd knock him down on his back and suck him under the wheels in the same position. This meant that the skull should've been shattered at the back. Now, supposedly it was possible that he had been hit from behind and turned over before the wheels crushed him, but then that would mean he had had *time* to turn around, and even if Dom had hit him there was no way he was malicious enough to stop, back up, *then* run him over. Vel scratched his chin that had itchy budding bumps at the bottom where hair was trying to grow in. Maybe he should've paid better attention in physics class, not that they specifically learned how speed and velocity changes the impact damage on a body. He just knew that nobody should've been able to damage the body in such a way with one go. There lied the real intent, knowing the victim, *wanting* this to happen.

He looked at Max Green's face, distorted and unpretty. The bruise from the tire slid off from his neck just past his ear, shearing the delicate flesh beneath. Vel blinked several more times, almost hallucinating Green blinking back at him with thin eyelids slipping over sinking grayed-out eyes. Swallowing a gulp of air that was mostly fresh but was becoming tainted by the body, he mustered the strength to stay standing over it instead of hurling in the trash bin. God forbid he proved Bosman right. Trying to keep his position, Vel brought his eyes back up to the cracked skull. Somehow that was so much easier to look at than the face proper. Once again he looked at the dust crusted into the blunt edges, then turned his head in curiosity. Sure, he had been hit next to a park, so dust from the park could've blown onto the road. But it didn't look like the asphalt of that road—the dust was too fine, too red instead of gray.

With a quick glance at the arguing adults, Vel ducked a hand into his pocket and tore off a small piece of the toilet paper wrapping he had taken from the cell. Gingerly he batted at the edge of the wound, trying to pick up dust on a dried clot of blood.

"Kid—what the *hell* are you doing?!"

"Um," Vel pulled the paper back into his hand, successful enough, "Souvenirs?"

"What the—you can't just—*hold on*,"

"I just don't know why his skull is cracked in front. Can you turn him over?" Vel said quickly, trying to move too fast so Bosman would get caught up in his own dumbfounded confusion.

"A skull can crack—he was *run over*, it doesn't matter how good you fall, you're gonna crack your damn skull open!"

"It *does* matter, doesn't it?" Vel said, arguing to keep his attention as he slipped the paper back into his pocket, "Because, if the front of his head shattered wouldn't that imply he got hit from behind?"

"*Potentially*, but—,"

"So what was he doing? Walking down the middle of the road early in the morning so that Dom could hit him from behind and run him over? Okay, but then why does the tire carve into his front side? Wouldn't that mean he'd have to flip himself over, or Dom would've had to back up and wait for him to move?"

"Kid—,"

"If he was crossing the street, wouldn't most of the impact be on his side? But I don't see a huge bruise on either side of him from the car grill. Or if he was hit in front, maybe the tire masks that, but wouldn't the skull be shattered in the back?"

"When bodies get hit by cars they go *kersplat*, you know! You can't exactly predict how they'll end up when they get knocked off their feet!"

"Okay but," Vel rubbed his chin again, "How much physics do you know? Dom usually goes the speed limit, and on that street it's only 25. Is that knock-off-your-feet-able? Y'know, enough to be thrown so far that worrying about where the skull breaks wouldn't matter?"

Bosman stared at Vel, fuming so hard he half-expected steam to come out of his ears. He turned to Sarge quick enough that Vel could feel the heat of it like a whip crack and snapped, "What goddamn parking lot did you pull him from?!"

"Don't tell my tía or she'll finally figure out where to return me," Vel bluntly pleaded.

Sarge soon hid her face in her pinched fingers. Frustrated, Bosman turned away and grumbled angrily that Vel didn't know what he was doing. Vel, indignant, stared at him all the while. Didn't know, huh? Then what was all this then? Surely he was doing well if he was pissing Bosman off like this.

"Bosman, just let him do it. Within reason."

"*He* doesn't know what he's *saying*," Bosman argued, "He hasn't a goddamn clue!"

Vel snorted, unoffended, "Can we turn him around?"

"Why," Bosman jeered, "Sick of looking at his face?"

Taking a glance at said face and swallowing the stomach churn, Vel confessed, "Yeah, actually."

"Alright, but you're helping."

"I am!" Vel said merrily, more than happy to be under his skin. Bosman glared.

"Remember you *don't* know what you're doing."

"Sure, sure," he deflected, wondering how long he could avoid being overtly offended, "How do we, uh,"

Grumbling the whole time and only enunciating to direct, Bosman helped turn the body on its stomach. It was both stiffer and limper than Vel expected, like a steak that hung out too long at the back of the fridge. He didn't know much about rigor mortis, but he had figured it had to settle in at some point, right? But then again the way that skeletons were found seemed to indicate that they grew limp again, probably during decomposition. There were so many questions to ask, but with Bosman's constant angry grumbling it didn't feel right to ask right then. Maybe he'd give his biology teacher a run for his money this week at school. But it wasn't like that was going to be much better, and the last thing he wanted was one of his classmates to overhear him asking how bodies died when his skin was brown enough to be called *terrorist* every so often at the grocery store. Perhaps the same one Bosman envisioned when he asserted that he had been adopted from its parking lot.

Green's arm laid unhealthily crooked over his backside, and Vel stared at it, wondering if he should pick it up or move it or even *how* to do so, if the bone would shift or the flesh would sag unpleasantly under his hands, or—and then Bosman flopped it off to the side. *Flump.* Audible. Vel stared at it, then shook his thoughts away and examined the back.

Overall it was stained purple, a result of blood pooling with gravity. Bosman indicated that the body was brought to him like that, the pooling at the back meaning he had been laying face up in the hours after he died. And yet, there were patches of torn skin across the lowest parts of his back and buttocks in the vague pattern of an elongated welt. All this bolstered Vel's suspicion that he was initially hit from behind. Still he squinted, perhaps tricking himself to see patterns in the way the skin tore. Patterns that would prove that it wasn't a minivan that had hit him. Anything to complicate the accusations thrown at his friends.

"What are you lookin' for, kid?"

"The...details, I guess," Vel said distantly as he peered at the dead skin.

"Cars really screw up a body. You'll get imprints, but what other details would you find or even need? You've already deduced some reasonable doubt."

Vel missed the compliment in his concentration. He didn't have gloves on, and every time he flexed his hand to touch skin he twitched and pulled back. It was not helped by the fact that he felt Bosman scrutinize his every move, especially when he brusquely pointed out that Vel was shaking. Meanwhile Sarge picked up where she had left off with more details about Max Green. He wasn't particularly rich despite the respect for him—although he was rumored to be looking to purchase land for a new botanical garden of local plants to preserve their necessity. Whether or not he had a grant or had struck a deal was anyone's guess. Since both his kids were still in college, there was potential for their bills to be larger than they expected and therefore money could've been tighter than rumors knew. Maybe it was insurance fraud, if his fervor for botanical preservation was strong enough. In the mundane details she listed height, weight, known abnormalities like a healed broken bone, latex allergy—

"Wait," Vel interrupted, struck by inspiration, "Wait, *wait*," he grabbed the clipboard from Sarge's hands. At first the words jumbled in their boxes and he had to acclimate to reading the chart. But it was there, clearly written: a latex allergy that caused swollen red rashes on the skin.

"I think—Hey, uh, doctor? Bosman? Do you have latex gloves around here?"

Bosman huffed, trying to figure out what the fuck he was thinking, "I do. Because no one else uses 'em so no one takes 'em from me."

Brightening, Vel was already moving to where his brain had subconsciously logged the glove boxes on the wall, "Perfect!"

"The body is *dead.* There's no blood pumping through the veins to react to an allergen, no blood to swell up and create a rash. What the hell are you doing?"

"Uh," Vel said, then decided to be too blunt to be real, "Magic."

Bosman shifted over to the sergeant and hissed, "K, what the hell is he doing?" To his frustration, Sarge had no answer as Vel snapped the gloves as far as they could reach down his wrists.

Gingerly, Vel brushed the skin on Green's back. Gave it a poke. He heard Bosman clear his throat with annoyance. For a while, nothing happened, and Vel shifted anxiously on his feet as the eager silence started to press down on his head. C'mon. *C'mon.* The water of his blood was still in there, it still remembered, it had to come out somehow. The air around Bosman was sucking inward, and Vel saw that his nose was tilting higher up in dismissal.

Then, the purple skin started to redden. Then puff up into clustered hives. Vel gently pressed the back of his fingers to the puffed skin, confirming a rash-like warmth. A beaming grin split his face and he turned towards Bosman and Sarge, "Look! *Latex allergy!*"

"No," Bosman grumbled as he stepped forward, "No, that ain't—,"

After his words cut themselves off at the sight of the rash, Vel jabbed, "Ain't what, old man?"

Even though his face soured there were no words left, and with a breath that sounded like a cat's hiss, Bosman turned on his heel and marched back to where Sarge was. Vel turned to Sarge, who didn't seem to much care if he continued or not. Bereft of emotive encouragement, Vel looked down at the body. Trying to frame the space of the impact point, he then started to lightly brush his fingers on Green's skin. Not deeply, not like a massage; Vel was trying to raise the skin that had been the least impacted, puffing it up to recreate the shape of the grill of the car that hit him. Before long it started to work, and at the backs of Green's legs the faint impression of the license plate even formed. It wasn't clear, but it was enough for Vel's heart to skip several beats in anticipation.

"Paint," he suddenly blurted, "You got paint, right?"

"*Paint?*" Bosman spat, "The hell do you think this is, a craft store?! No, we don't have any paint!"

Vel tried ignoring him, "Gonna need a big sheet of paper too. To stamp this impression on it."

Bosman started cussing as he moved boxes despite himself, or perhaps to prove to Vel in no uncertain terms that they had nothing of the sort in his morgue. Vel watched for a while in muted interest, once or twice flinching at the angry speed that Bosman shunted something aside.

"Don't you dress the bodies up or something?" Vel said, "Like, with makeup?" It was a tentative attempt at smugness;

he was glad to be under Bosman's skin in the same way he had tripped up Sarge, but was intimidated more than he cared to admit.

"We're not a goddamn funeral home," Bosman snapped, "As for paper, you're gonna have to tape pieces from the printer together if you want to cover his whole backside."

Unfortunately for Bosman, it didn't matter to Vel so long as he could do it. Whether or not that was petty, the medical examiner certainly took it as such by the glint in the glare he shot at Vel.

"So start taping!" he yelled.

Vel turned around looking for a printer but found none, still asking, "What about paint, or ink?"

"We don't *have* any!"

Sarge shifted on her feet and Vel looked over just in time to see a decision finalize on her face. There was a pointed look at Bosman to witness his reaction, and suddenly Vel got the impression that behind Sarge's stone façade she was just as interested in getting one up on the ornery old man, "Toner."

Something in Bosman truly snapped. It was the angriest disbelief Vel had ever seen this side of his tía. Just like her, the disbelief was to no avail. No, it was truly a unique sort of despair on Bosman's face and while Sarge looked mildly pleased Vel was observing him in utter fascination.

After several moments of Bosman's unresolved anger, Vel, clueless, asked, "Does toner stain?"

"Not permanently." Sarge answered.

Gruff, flustered, and gritting his teeth, Bosman corrected her with, "Your pride, yes." Vel surmised that there were multiple meanings to that statement.

Half an hour later he had taped printer paper into a large

sheet while the adults pulled a cartridge of waste toner from the office. Bosman was bickering on the losing side of a battle but kept doing so regardless. The fact that Sarge said next to nothing in turn cemented her victory in Vel's mind, and she handed the box of jet-black dust to him.

"*Don't* drop it."

"How bad would it be?" he asked, never having touched an office-grade printer in his life.

"I said *don't drop it.*" Sarge reiterated without answering him.

"Sheesh." Vel muttered, suddenly extremely tempted to drop it on the crisp bleach-white floors.

Careful despite the raging temptation in his heart, Vel smeared the toner on the latex rash like he was preparing a rubber stamp. Bit by bit the general impression of the car's grill became clear, and when enough of Green's backside had been covered he picked up the sheet of paper. Shaking it out like a rug and pressing it gently to the body, he rubbed it smooth. There was a deep knotted hope in his heart that he could almost call a prayer, were he not allergic to anything his tía tried to impede on him. Regardless he leaned into the feeling without giving it a name and slowly peeled the paper back. When he laid it flat on the floor all three of them peered over the impression.

"That's not a Chrysler emblem," Vel murmured, staring at the center of the car's grill, "Not like the one on Dom's van."

"I guess it could be a sedan," Bosman grunted.

Glancing up, Vel took a chipper shot at him, "Good enough?"

Bosman huffed and turned to rinse the toner off as if it hadn't done anything at all.

9

"K, give me a moment with the kid."

Vel bristled. Toner was still smeared on his wrists. Overhear-ing that made him turn the lab's faucet on quick to pretend that he was none the wiser—maybe even too busy for a chat, if he could knock it. For all his smugness, he was wary of Bosman like he was wary of his teachers. If they couldn't punish him, they would at least make him feel terrible about the job he had done. Even if he knew his answer was correct, the anxiety in delivering it would screw him up enough that a teacher's impatience could ruin it all together. At least with them he had designated subjects to draw responses from his memory banks. Here, though, anything could've been on Bosman's mind and that made Vel scrub his skin harder even though the toner slipped right off. Sarge honored Bosman's request and left the lab, and Vel sunk his head between his shoulders for meager protection.

"Kid," Bosman started. There was a pause and it was unclear if he was waiting for Vel's acknowledgment or he was trying to conjure a name. Regardless of what he really wanted, he continued with the latter, "What's your name?"

"Vel." he answered without looking up. His voice was guarded in an absent way; walled off but trying to play it as

93

normal. Bosman gave a one-note laugh. Vel readied himself for mockery.

"Wise guy in every way possible, huh?" Vel looked over at him with a blank yet apprehensive stare. Vel was what everyone called him, what he wanted to be called, and it was going to be kinder to hear Bosman sneer and make fun of Vel rather than something like Jerónimo. But instead of that he sighed, releasing a weight. That weight was still tied to Bosman in a startling way, the release more about letting the tightened curtain fall rather than getting rid of a heavy load.

"Kid," he said again, lower, more serious, "Are you sure you wanna poke your nose into this?"

Offended to his core but too wary to show it, Vel clamped down on the insides of his cheeks, "I have to do this."

Bosman twisted his mouth, "You aren't thinking about becoming an investigator or something are you?" It was probing. Vel shrugged, having no good answer for his future even though graduation was around the corner. Bosman looked away and idly tapped the edge of the sink. Each tap echoed through the stainless steel basin, a noise easy to latch onto while anxiety ripped through him, "Still, getting yourself involved in all this alone...,"

"My friends are in trouble." Vel interrupted defiantly. To his complete and utter shock, Bosman's expression saddened as he stared right through him.

"That's the crux of it all, ain't it?"

Vel scrunched his face, catching that Bosman meant something more but couldn't figure what. Frustration bubbled in his throat, angry that he wasn't wise enough and angrier still that he felt he *could* be if he had just had the answers that eluded him.

"Hey, kid. Vel. Why are they listening to *you*, of all people?"

He shrugged again, but it was becoming terrifyingly clear that he wasn't fooling Bosman.

"*C'mon*," Bosman scoffed, "You know better. They're setting you all up."

The frustration roiled. Vel *knew* that and it didn't help that Bosman needled him for knowing that. He felt his frown pull his mouth into a bitter snarl that reflected that frustration and snipped, "What choice do I have? Even if I don't play their game, I lose."

"You could lose a hell of a lot less if you stay out of it."

What hurt more than anything else was that Bosman's reply was so quick it was clear he didn't even have to think about it. Meanwhile Vel *had* to think and think hard. Yet for all his thinking in the silence he couldn't draw a different conclusion. In his mind there was his mother's body jutting into the light from the hallway, her hand curled over something he couldn't see and gleaming darkly. Slipping off into nothingness, Vel shook his head. Slightly, then more and more as he tried to rid himself of the gruesome image.

"I can't," he rasped in protest, "I still lose. I'd rather try."

Bosman inhaled, looked at Vel, looked like there was something he wanted to say. The exhale came without a word.

"I guess that's nothin' but the truth, huh," he finally said after a long, long, while. The words held an untold weight behind them. Vel knew he wasn't going to be able to place them but he tried anyway. There was a sudden sorrow to Bosman's eyes that gave them the uncomfortable texture of age and knowledge. Then he said, "Are you sure this is the job for you?"

"Like...career?" Vel clarified. Bosman nodded and Vel thought about it, "I dunno. Dunno what else I got going for me.

I guess...if I'm good at this, why not?"

Bosman looked as though he had backed into his own trap, then with resignation spoke practically, "It's all just a den of snakes. Not just the people, but the mentality you have to have. You start looking at people and judging them by the harm they *could* do, which makes you believe it's the harm they *would* do. You grow bitter and cold and don't look at bodies the same way. Almost wish you would've thrown up, 'cause it would've reminded me how real this all actually is."

Defiant and petty, Vel narrowed his eyes, "But do you *have* to be that way?"

At that Bosman twisted his mouth into a half-smile, half-grimace, "Well I guess I only had the one shot to see."

Vel felt his guard lower, seeing Bosman's age as more than just bitter and asocial. Shaking his hands in the sink, he watched water droplets spray against the stainless steel into violent constellations.

"I don't know," Vel finally answered him, "But if what I do helps, I want to do it."

A ghost of a genuine smile tugged at the corner of his lips, "That's what I'm afraid of. So long as you're here, K is a stick in the mud but a good one. Stay close to her. I mean it."

"She seems fun to annoy." Vel commented dryly.

"*God Jesus lord almighty* I did not have kids for a reason." Bosman grumbled under his breath.

"Why not?"

"I pray you never find out."

Bosman left the room but Vel stayed at the sink, letting his words mull in his mind. They didn't fit the way Vel had expected them to. Bosman felt like the kind of person his teachers proclaimed to be. Barbed on the outside but genuinely caring on the inside. That being said, he was having a very hard time believing that Bosman's care was real. Not that it was *faked*, but Vel had no notion that someone *would* care so recklessly. In Church it was pounded into his head over and over again, love thy neighbor, care for the destitute, look out for each other, however it was preached from the scripture to the contemporary word. But that's where the dichotomy rested: Everything in the Church walls seemed correct, everything outside seemed to contradict. His tía cared about him; out of obligation, out of genuine love, out of faith to the Church, and still Vel could never look at her as *caring*. As for what happened at school where teachers proclaimed his importance and denounced his efforts in the same breath, well, the Church could say whatever they wanted. Why did Bosman care about him? The world didn't work like that.

But maybe Bosman knew that and was making a conscious effort against the pressures around him. It was still hard to grapple that it was for Vel's sake, but it sounded...right. It sounded mature. It sounded real.

Like a holy smiting pang, his head burst realizing he had done *no* homework *and* from here he was about to go straight home. No longer concerned with the curiosity that was Bosman, Vel took two steps to the door and stopped.

Turned.

The open cartridge of toner was set upon one of the rolling trays. If he tipped it like a spiteful cat it'd clatter and shroud him in guilt. But if he found a way to feign plausible deniability, then the cat could have its curiosity and eat it, too.

Creeping close, Vel reached out and nudged the cartridge. Further. A little further. And...just enough. Not for it to topple off, not right away, but the threat was there. Feeling a rush of satisfaction, he bit down on his mischievous grin and left the room.

Sarge and Bosman looked at him, scrutinizing in a way that he could tell they had been talking. It was too obvious to hide it, but they didn't look awkward about it either. Though they didn't divulge anything, he knew he'd probably figure it out on his own come time and reflection. For now he had to go home.

A loud, catastrophic clatter destroyed the mutual silence and Bosman's eyes closed in despair before he burst into colorful curse words. Fingers digging into his scalp, he stomped back into the lab. Vel innocently craned his neck to see a black explosion in the shape of a star. Its blackness was so dark he couldn't see light reflected in it, and the realization of just how bad of a mess it was made him gleeful in his mischief. The door swung closed and he chanced a glance at Sarge, who narrowed her eyes. Vel clapped a hand over his mouth so it wouldn't be *too* obvious he was utterly elated.

"See you in court?" he said bouncily.

Sarge rolled her eyes and led him out of the building to the cadence of Bosman's muffled swearing.

Vel ducked and stumbled through the front door that seemed shorter and shorter every year. When his tía agreed to care for him she left her convent all together, nabbing a small two-bedroom rental home that had the structure of a trailer despite not actually being one. The walls were filled to the corners with either bloodied Jesus slumping on the cross or shimmering images of Virgen de Guadalupe; opulent displays of worship and protection. True that Vel didn't know if she had taken a vow of poverty as a nun, but if her opulence was used to show how devout her heart was then she certainly allowed herself that. There was always a scent in the air of the small rectangular home, either from dried desert flowers, lit candles, or cooking food. It was the latter-most when Vel came home, sofrito flavoring both chicken and rice. Vel's stomach roared and he bee-lined to the kitchen not so much from gratitude but necessity.

As to be expected even though he wished she were somewhere else, Tía Gloria was there, heat-resistant hands gripping cast-iron handles with nothing more than a mere towel. She was similar to his mother in that she was stocky, had light skin, and dark curly hair. That was where the similarities ended. While his mother's eyes had a warmth to their darkness (and that darkness was at times attributed to more than just their color), the warmth that Tía Gloria showed was to the world outside of her nephew. Her outward generosity did touch him—he was here, after all, and not in a boys' home—but he couldn't escape the scrutiny of a family schism he had no hope to untangle. The other marked difference, the one that hurt the most for Vel to see, was the age on her skin. Tía Gloria had been the elder sister, sure, but whether by his youth or the shortness of her life he did not remember crow's feet, burgeoning liver spots, and flabby elbows on his mother's body. Hard to tell if he resented his tía for that. Of course it wasn't her *fault*, but it wasn't fair either.

"Ah-*ah!*" she slapped his hand with a wooden spoon, "Did you learn your lesson?"

"*Ow*," Vel hissed and shook his hand dramatically, but pulled a plate from the cupboard regardless, "Not the lesson you wanted me to learn!"

"You never do," she glowered. The food she was cooking simmered to match her temper. Both things enticed Vel just the same. Tipping the lid off of the chicken enveloped him in a warm, delicious smell of aromatics stewed deep into the meat. In his peripheral vision he saw her nose turn up at the sound of his stomach; proud at her handiwork's effect on him, piercing that he felt so free to take it without gratitude or grace. *Especially* after the weekend he put himself through.

"Isn't that what a teenager is supposed to do?" he snarkily replied, earning another rap of the spoon on his hand. The cover for the chicken clattered onto the skillet and Vel yelped at the splashed condensation from the lid, "Oh my g—," quick, stop, swallow that word, keep going even though she raised an eyebrow, "What do you want me to *do??*"

Wrong question. Tía Gloria fixed her posture to perfection

and Vel at once knew he had invited the avalanche on himself, "The choir was counting on you to perform, and yet when the time came there was only empty air where you should've been standing,"

"Oh please," Vel grumbled, knocking the lid away from the chicken to serve himself two of the five breasts she had prepared, "A hole in the farthest of far back rows, they can make do."

"An empty seat next to me throughout all of Mass. The floor isn't swept. The house isn't dusted. And your homework! Did you do your homework in that *jail cell?* You have *responsibilities*, you know!"

Half of those are responsibilities you want *me to have*, he thought sourly, smart enough to not say it out loud. He wasn't, however, smart enough to keep the next thought inside, "Did you bring me my homework to do while I was there?"

He reached for the rice slow enough for her to aim the spoon again, jerking just out of the way so it slapped the lid with a sharp noise. While she was startled he quickly heaped yellow rice onto his plate.

"You *had* the opportunity to come home, and you threw it away yourself!" she snapped upon recovering. Vel shrugged.

"It was more important."

"*Nothing* is more important than your education!"

Vel fell deathly silent, a clear indication that he was not playing games just as much as she wasn't. All he could think of were the ensuing weeks after his mother's death, curled tight in his middle school desk and trying to let the teacher's words take him away but failing to concentrate. Was that his fault? If his tía believed in the salvation of sinners, then her assertion that he was shaping out to be an irreversible failure was a curious one.

"I dunno," he said, skewering in his casualness, "I think your sister was pretty important."

"*Jerónimo por Dios—,*"

"I'm hungry." he said plainly, lifting his plate over her head to maneuver out of the cramped kitchen to the equally cramped table with one side shoved flush to the wall. He sat so the kitchen was in his view through the tiny bar piled with mail and bagged potatoes. His tía was further partially obscured by the hanging garlic knots and dried chiles, but he could tell that the steam in the kitchen was more the fumes of her anger than her cooking. He heard a couple of tortillas slap onto the comal, feeling the dangerous dark of her gaze without seeing it. Before long she slammed a warmer with a couple of fresh tortillas inside onto the table, and Vel reached for one mid-chew.

When she spoke again her voice was leveled and low, meaning that what he had said had gotten through to her. That was good. But. He still never knew if *getting through* meant it hurt in the way he felt it should've. Regardless, he'd take his victories where he could.

"You have to think of the *here and now*, Jeró," she set home-knit hotpads down for the chicken and rice, off-color and toughened from use, "Not the past."

"Should I think of the future, then?" he asked through a mouthful.

"It'd be nice if you did." she shot. Vel chewed.

"Well, I am," he said, "I'm thinking of how to get my friends out of jail."

Tía Gloria sighed, exasperated, "*Your* future—,"

"They *are* my future!" Vel argued, not caring if he sounded like a stupid high schooler that put too much import upon silly, ethereal things.

"*Jerónimo—,*"

"Fine, *part* of my future, then! What's so bad about that?" He didn't care about high school things like prom or graduating, really. Just his friends and a future with them in his life—even if they aged away from each other in the end. So long as he had the option to pick up the phone and have them be there, that was the future he was vying for, "Besides, they're letting me on the case and everything. Why *wouldn't* I take the chance?"

Tía Gloria stared at him with an expression he was sure he'd never seen before. Something close to real concern, unclouded by her own resentment for him and how she rationalized her sister's decisions. It didn't make him falter—if anything he was bitterly glad he had finally pulled some semblance of real care from her brutalizing façade.

Despite her surprising expression, though, her words were just as wrong as ever, "Because they'll be able to live without you. You need to care for yourself outside of them. Eat, do your homework, and straight to bed."

Boiling hot oil bubbled in Vel's stomach up to his eyes, and too late he realized he was on the verge of crying tears of rage. That wasn't the point. That wasn't the *point.*Another tortilla, filled to spilling with rice and chicken. He stuffed his face. His tía had not yet sat down, manning the comal for more fresh tortillas to make up for the ones lost to Vel's stomach. She had not made five chicken breasts for leftovers. Only one would go to her, but the vacuous pit that was his tall teenager stomach would consume everything else. They were both used to it. Vel stuffed his face in a desperate attempt to reach an equilibrium he could cling to lest he pick up his plate and fling it into the wall.

More tortillas into the warmer, more tortillas on the comal, she still had yet to sit. His stomach was slowly filling and yet it never felt more hollow.

Through a voice that cracked more from tears than from youth, Vel mumbled when she was in earshot, "You're not my mom."

The silence was deafening. Tía Gloria stared at him, cold, damning, resentful. Then she turned on her heel and returned to the comal.

Maybe, maybe she was saying these things because deep down she actually didn't want to lose him too. Maybe, maybe she was afraid he'd be the one in trouble in place of his friends. Maybe, maybe she really did care. He wanted to love his Tía Gloria. But she made it impossible, so he made himself impossible to care for. Whether that was to test her or punish her, he didn't know. Did it matter?

Vel went to his room with his stomach full but still he felt hungry.

11

Homework. Homework was important. He knew that. Emotionally he didn't think he could handle another snide or disappointed sneer from his teachers that were already used to his empty hands. It didn't feel good to feel stupid even if he pretended not to care. So do the homework now to avoid everything else later. It'd be easier.

But god. Goddammit. He opened his precalculus textbook and the numbers swelled like a latex allergy before falling off the page. English homework—he read the words in Dom's voice that quickly melted into telling him what had, or hadn't, happened. Social studies—what did past justices matter when Sebbie was scared behind bars?

Vel shoved it away and fell back against the side of his bed with a harrowed sigh. Pressing his face into his hands until he saw red, he scraped his heels on the shitty carpet.

He needed permission. Wait. No. No he didn't. He was almost an adult anyway, and an adult could do whatever they wanted, right? Truthfully if he was straddling the gap between youth and adulthood he should be allowed a few selfish decisions, even if reckless. Did Sarge and Bosman really expect him to go and be a good little student with all this hanging over his head? He looked to the dark gap under his bed. Would his mother?

Suddenly Vel snorted. His mother had a whole life that she ditched in Mexico for the sake of her son, right? He could ditch homework for *one* week for the sake of his friends.

Clearing his bedroom floor, Vel emptied his pockets and spread the map of Tucson out. Wrapped in single-ply toilet paper was the chip of paint from the jail bars and tiny clumps of dusty blood from Max Green. Next to those he laid the two discarded sucker wrappers, same brand, same black cherry flavor. (The sucker that still had its candy disappeared into his mouth despite finding it in the dirt.)And...that was it. This was more the collection of a weird kleptomaniac than a pile of evidence. Puffing out his cheeks, he gave his room a once-over for help.

It was modest and small, smaller still that he was outgrowing everything within it both literally and figuratively. His feet hung over the bed frame and had already rubbed the edges bare. The few stuffed animals his mother had salvaged from a garage sale were on his dresser, raggedy and balding in spots; some of which he remembered from when the toys were new to him. The dresser he had started to pick at as soon as he moved in with his tía, chips of the wood scraped away sometimes to form obscenities, sometimes just to have the power to change something in his environment. There were a few cardboard boxes that still remained from the move, mostly holding trinkets and things he had saved for one reason or another once he was old enough to roam the neighborhood on his own. Odd sticks, pretty rocks, an animal bone, cactus spines, and a particularly decent collection of arrowheads all sat in a lining of paper towels regardless of the legality of keeping them. (Not owning, no, that felt wrong to say somehow, but he couldn't parse why.) The walls were filled with drawings from

Sebbie, the drawers bursting with spent character sheets from Dom. Something hurt beneath the heart when his eyes fell on those.

Stumped even still, Vel looked at the map of Tucson. He tried to let his mind fall blank with the distraction of finding the park he drove Sebbie past. Pulling out a marker he placed an X over it, then with his scrawny fingers walked the direction the roadrunner had taken them until he approximated where the abandoned parking lot was. Another X, and he leaned back to see just how far one was from the other. It was a hell of a ways as the crow flies, not to mention by car.

Vel took another glance around the room, then grabbed two stuffed animals off his dresser. One was a beat up dog that was probably a wolf but he had always called a coyote, the other a rabbit. Predator and prey, or murderer and victim. To exemplify this he carefully wedged a crust of Green's blood into the threadbare forehead of the rabbit. Now to recreate the scene. He placed the rabbit on the X over the park, put the toy car in front of it, and the coyote behind the car. And...

Nothing.

He waited. Still nothing.

Surely something should've happened. Some sort of clue, even if that clue was telling him he was going about this all wrong.

But no, nothing.

Frustration threatened to bubble in him. A whole weekend of things working out, though not in the way he expected, and now *this?* His friends *needed* him! Granted he didn't even know what he was trying to find out, but something should've helped. Something. *Anything.* He reached forward and nudged the rabbit, nudged the car into the rabbit's feet. No dice. Trying to stay calm, Vel clamped his hands over his ears and applied pressure, staring at the staged scene until the details went blurry. He couldn't conjure anything of course, that's not how it worked and he'd said as much. But that couldn't just mean that this was all...nothing, either. Because someone was dead, his friends were taking the fall, *something* had to have happened.

"*Ugh!*" Vel spat, and if his tía had asked he would've told her it was just precalc—something she couldn't help with. Giving up, he picked up the sucker wrappers and decided to figure that mystery out instead. He placed one on either head of the stuffed animals, disappointed when they fell at the slightest agitation. Vel grumbled, taking the wrapper off of the coyote's head and licking the inside of it before he thought about the debris.

"C'mon you bastards, I know it's one of you," he muttered bitterly, slapping the wrapper back on the coyote. Still nothing, and Vel slid it around to its mouth until suddenly the wrapper stuck. Startled, Vel pulled, ripping the paper in two. Excited simply because *something* was working, he picked at the stuck wrapper, peeling it back to reveal half-melted black cherry candy gunking up the coyote's mouth. Excitement wavered into miffed annoyance, because now he had to pick the candy out of its fur. Well, fine, that was sign enough that the murderer was the one that liked black cherry suckers, putting him at both the park and the abandoned theater. At the expense of his poor coyote. Well, he supposed magic did have its sacrifices.

A wheezing screech split his ears and Vel jumped back away from the sound, crunching himself against his bed. The coyote hung limp from his hands, and in his panic his eyes focused on too much and nothing at once until they saw the rabbit. He must've pushed it over the X on the parking lot—or at least that's what he assumed, because what he saw instead was the rabbit twisted over itself like it had bones that had snapped. In fact, the same arm that was broken on Green was distorted on the rabbit in the same way. Its knitted eyes were twice as faded, pale, deathly so. Between those eyes the head split from a fracture, stuffing bursting out of the fabric in a ghastly manner. Vel's lip hung open, trying to form a thought out loud. The toy car was just beyond the rabbit's body, as though it had run it over.

Then, there was the smell of copper. Pungent. Fresh. Damning. Vel watched in horror as blood seeped out of the rabbit's ripped stitching, pooling and sinking into the map beneath it. More blood flowed. More. As much as there would've been in a human's body, surely—that was the thought that sprung to his mind seconds before he panicked.

"*Jeró? What was that?! ¡¿Estás bien?!*" his tía was there in an instant, spiking his throat as her knuckles rapped frantically on his door. Fully aware that she could hear him, Vel crumpled the map over everything and shoved it under his bed.

"N-Nothing!" his voice cracked on its own breathlessness, "I'm—fine!"

The smell of blood seared his nostrils, especially so that his hands were red from the soaked map. Thinking far too quickly to actually *think*, Vel jammed the side of his palm against a jagged edge of his dresser. Clamping his teeth on his lips, Vel inhaled sharp as dark red globs beaded and burst down his hand. Just in time, too, because his tía opened his door with the unneeded force of her shoulder. Vel flinched, still seated on his carpet floor.

"¿Estás bien?" she asked again, eyes wide. Vel, unable to form words, looked at her dumbly. Her nostrils flared and the worry in her eyes intensified, "That—That's blood, I smell blood!"

"Y-Yeah, I," Vel's mind raced, "I cut my hand trying to get a pencil."

She shook her head, "There's a *lot* of blood,"

"It's just—," he knew he sounded scared at best and only hoped that worked in his favor, "Small room. I'll open a window."

He awkwardly reached for the window above his bed, trying to use his body to hide what he had quickly shoved underneath. He felt his tía's eyes on him the whole time, and from both that and the rabbit's death knell screech his hands were shaking. Forcing the rickety window open, he flopped back down on the floor and looked up at her. She looked back. Fearing that she was seeing right through him, Vel tried to force a shaky scowl.

"Told ya homework is deadly."

Tía Gloria scrutinized him. Vel swallowed hard, overtly aware of his recently protruding Adam's apple bobbing with it.

"What homework?" she asked, skewering. Biting his inner cheek to try and stop any tells, he looked over to where he had shoved all his books.

"Well, nothing yet. I hurt myself. Don't wanna bleed over that precalc book or they'll make me keep it."

"...Show me." she said, her voice wary but the relief just as obvious. Vel offered his busted hand, two creeks of blood wrapping around his wrist down his arm from the wound. Tía Gloria cooed as she crouched to examine it and Vel felt his heart pound, pressing himself tighter against his bed. To his relief, she said, "Come to the bathroom." and turned around without noticing anything.

If nothing else she was very good at patching *physical* wounds up. Vel waited patiently and quietly as she did so, which must've been a surprising change for him. As such she didn't complain in turn, although he wondered how suspicious he was being. Then again, it *had* been a rough weekend, and maybe in the end his tía's suspicion was subdued because of everything that had happened. He watched her weathered thumbs smooth over the thick bandage, dutifully bent down to receive a kiss, then slunk his way back to his room. He was numb, numb with dull panic. Not that he feared for his life, or feared anything, but it was similar to seeing Green's mangled body for the first time. Death that wasn't an immediate danger to him, just a sublimely mundane reminder of fragility in all its gruesomeness. With the door closed behind him he knelt down and slid the bundle out from under his bed.

To both his relief and confusion, the blood had dried. Actually, as he unwrapped the map, he realized the blood had consolidated on the abandoned parking lot before drying. In the deepest center of the pool was the other sucker wrapper, soaked so thoroughly it stuck to the map. It felt significant in a different way; of course the killer was the one who killed the victim, but how thoroughly the wrapper was stuck made him think that the parking lot was more important than just convenience. He thought over what Sarge had said of the theater, how it was slowly abandoned over time. Did that mean it still had an owner? Was it looking for a new owner, or, if it already had one, why was it sitting abandoned? Surely not to be a hotspot for murder; Sarge would've pointed out its connections to other victims. Vel scratched his head. Beyond that, why were the killer and the victim in that parking lot at the same time anyway?

Hell, maybe it really was just drug deals or horny backseat fucks.

As his panic faded, exhaustion overwhelmed him. Re-wrapping all of the evidence, he gave a quiet vigil to both his stuffed animals before pushing them far under his bed. He was going to be alright, magic had its sacrifices, but he felt a strange melancholy that the top of his dresser was barer than before. Sure, it looked more adult, he supposed. But part of him wasn't exactly ready to say good-bye yet and he hadn't thought that he was going to have to. Nevermind so violently. Crawling into bed, he pulled his last remaining plushie off of the dresser. He was almost sure it was the lion from the D.A.R.E. program and thus he didn't blame a kid for putting it out in a garage sale. But he valued it now, laughing at the irony of how he had already been smoking for a year before pressing it to his chest until his heartbeat calmed enough to sleep.

12

Gym class was worse than usual. Sure, it *was* a basketball unit, and for the past week or so all Vel had to do was stand near the basket and put a hand up if anyone got close to it, more akin to a goalie than anything else. It was something he was at least good at and didn't have to strain his knees that badly—but it had its cost. The teacher, a short woman who was flat, wiry, and mean, often shouted at him to move regardless of his knee braces. This invigorated the other students, teammate and rival alike, to badger him to 'pull his weight'. More than once his sloppy coordination with his growing arms and bandaged hand knocked a passed ball away, but they kept passing it to him. Incessantly. Like they were forcing him to abscond the advantage of his height like he didn't already know he was a bad player. There was no Sebbie, whom he shared the hour with, to take the blows alongside him. While not too athletic, he was quick and darting enough to steal the ball away from it ever contacting Vel.

It was something the two usually joked about in the locker rooms; the short guy was the basketball player, the tall guy more suited to just holding the net up and waiting for several impromptu facelifts. The irony wasn't lost on his fellow classmates, but it stung more when they snapped at him, making him fumble harder, making them snap more. It didn't help that his mind was not in the game nor even remotely in the same building, setting him up for more than one collision that knocked his knees out and had him seething in pain on the court. Ms. Patton would then shout at him for not moving out of the way, or fouling for illegal defending (whatever *that* meant), forcing him to get back up and in the game without assessing any damage. He was the tall guy, right. He had to be the one good at basketball, so suited to the sport that he was expected to take all the blows and difficulties as if it was built into his bones, right.

Vel hunched his shoulders in the locker room and tried to keep himself unremarkable. He had not kept track of if they had won or lost any of the games they played; he had only heard the constant jeers and shouts from either side with no Sebbie to distract him with jokes or otherwise.

A shove came at his shoulder that was too harsh to be accidental and Vel looked up. Usually it was only one or two, but now *five* other boys crowded at his side. There was a gleam in their eyes that Vel didn't like, and immediately his blood pumped hard, knowing there was nowhere to run.

"Hey Geronimo, what's the height for if you can't play basketball for shit?" the foremost one said. His name was Mitch Winters, easily recognized and avoided by all three of them for good reason. What made him worse was that he was *smart*, really smart, like a goddamn sponge. Adult notions that breadth of knowledge equated to empathy were completely squashed whenever Mitch Winters opened his mouth. Vel kept his gaze steady, both on prey instinct and also on the off-chance that the eye contact would be unsettling enough that he'd back down. Even with Vel's sharp and unique eyes, though, with a big group backing him up there'd be nothing to deter him and Vel knew it, "Or does your little gay boyfriend do all the work in the relationship?"

"Yeah maybe," Vel said, level and trying to seem unaffected. To his growing anxiety, his strategy didn't do anything. The boys hooted like it was an admission of guilt and they were judge, jury, and executioner. One kicked at his shin, a definitive warning beneath the knee brace.

"So what happened? Did you lose at limp biscuit and your other two dipshit friends ran away together?" Winters sneered, his voice dripping with poisoned honey.

"Um," Vel gasped, unable to argue back. If he'd said the truth it'd either damn him or be twisted to damn him anyway. Besides, give them the ammo that they were jailed on suspicion of *murder* and the logic Winters was following would be *worse*.

"You know what was written into Arizona law before it became a state?" Winters was getting close enough that Vel could smell the sharp minty gum hiding the chew on his breath and he tried not to wrinkle his nose. He *did* pay attention in history; history and similar subjects to it were the only things Vel could grasp onto with any ease. Something about digging into the records of the land made him think of his mother, and beyond that he liked learning about how Tucson grew into the city it was today—or rather, how Tucson had always been here as far back as anyone can remember. Its roots seemed so deep that they certainly had a place for his own as well, and despite how shitty his life had been there was an entrenching love for the city that was both tangibly and intangibly home.

But he didn't know what Winters was talking about. They had an assignment due at the end of the semester, sure; researching a point or topic in Arizona's history and contrasting it with how it compared nationally. It was clear that Winters had chosen something based in law, but that was as far as Vel got. Winters knew it, and a cruel smirk pushed up one of his cheeks, "Fags got life in prison."

"I'm not—," Vel protested. He wasn't interrupted, no. Horribly he couldn't choke the words out. Not because they weren't true, but because it was getting hard to speak at all.

"Hey bud, don't worry about it," he slapped Vel's arm like a teammate would and Vel flinched, "Some good ol' exposure therapy'd clear it up, right?"

Vel opened his mouth to ask what the hell he meant but before more than a sound could get out Winter's hand closed hard on his arm. Then the boys were on him, wrenching him off the bench in a painful tangle between his legs and the wood. Before Vel could flail and scamper away another stinging pain shot up from his knees and he howled. Someone stuffed a sweaty sock in his mouth to shut him up and tears sprung to his eyes from the nasty funk. Briefly he thought of Bosman's quippy comment. Though he was mostly immune to his own stench he couldn't deny that the sock in his mouth was *foul*. Fouler than the porn-stuffed shoebox under his bed. It sent stars to his eyes, and in the resulting blindness he felt his body quartered between the bullies and dragged away. The locker door swung open to a blast of chilled hallway air. For a while he just let it happen as his legs tingled, planning his escape as soon as they threw him out.

Then another door was shouldered open and too late horror dawned on Vel. He was met with a blast of warm air, but not from outside. No, it was similarly musty to the boys' locker room but different; permeated with flowery perfume and lotion and unfamiliar scents and between that and the sock in his mouth he felt dizzy. Vel tried to pinwheel his limbs backward, pulling his legs free enough to dig his heels into the tile floor, the horror crowning with the realization that he was in his boxers. The boys flung him into the girls' locker room with cackling glee that became muffled the second they slammed the door. Screams erupted around him and his eyes saw rows and rows of bare legs before he shut them with a cracked shriek of his own.

"*No, wait!*" he shouted as the screams reached an echoing cacophony in the tiled room. Blind, he scrambled backward, hit the wall, cried out again, and pawed for the door. When his hands found it and pushed, however, it didn't budge. The cackling on the other side intensified and Vel understood that all five boys were bracing the door shut. Still he desperately tried to shoulder it open. He was tall, he had leverage, he slammed his shoulder against it over and over again to little avail.

To make matters worse, something hit him and clattered to the floor. It wasn't large or heavy, but it stung deeper than its impact. Chancing a glance he saw someone's chapstick roll away into the corner. Vel scrunched his eyes shut again as more things started to hit him. Perhaps they didn't *hurt* hurt. But he desperately, deeply wished they'd stop all the same. All the girls were shouting at him to leave as if he had any power, accusing him of being a pervert even though he was tucking his head into his shoulders like a whipped dog.

"*Let me out!*" he wailed, "Goddammit, *hey!!*" His head swam from all the noise, knowing the boys on the other side of the door were taunting him while he heard the girls do much the same with accosted anger. Vel started banging on the door frantically, hoping to add urgency to his plight to anybody that would've heard and helped.

"*Velasquez!*"

Well. Ms. Patton certainly heard. The *helped* part was yet to be determined. She emerged from her office connected to the locker room and though Vel knew he should've looked he cowered against the door and refused to.

"*What* are you doing in the *girls' locker room?!*"

"Nothing!" Vel protested, "Mitch Winters and his goons threw me in here!"

"Oh?" she sneered, "And you need someone to help you *leave* the locker room?"

"They're holding the door shut!"

Ms. Patton gave a very condescending sigh before taking two steps forward to test the door. It swung open with ease, so much so that when Vel's eyes opened in shock he found that no one was there; the boys had left either back to their locker room or to where students congregated waiting for the bell. Cold washed over him and sank deep as he realized just how much trouble he was in.

"Ms. Patton—," he choked, "*Really!* Why would I barge in without pants?!"

Her eyes narrowed and Vel swallowed hard. In the past weekend he had never felt more like an adult, taken seriously by both a police sergeant and a medical examiner despite his hare-brained investigations. Here he realized the curse of still being treated like one, because he couldn't argue that he was still a kid—seventeen was a bit too old to genuinely put forth an argument of cooties. On top of everything else, when he scraped himself to his feet he was well over Ms. Patton's height. What, was he stupid for letting himself be overpowered? The narrowing of her eyes then appeared to him to be less of an adult's disappointment and more that she was gauging him as a *threat.* Hunching over helped nothing. Vel tried protesting again, weak and short of breath.

"*Please.*"

"*You* are going to be lucky if they *don't* suspend you." she snarled, dark and chilling. Panic started to set in as her nails dug into his arm to drag him to the office regardless of his pantslessness. A locker room full of girls seeing his boxers was bad enough, sure, why not parade him around the whole school? He was so tall that his junk would be at eye level for everyone eating in the cafeteria. The noise Vel's throat made when he sucked in air through his open mouth made him dizzy.

"*Wait,*" he protested again, still unable to find words. How the hell could he carry conversation with dutiful professionals over a dead body but shrivel up when he *actually* really needed it?

"Ms. Patton," one of the girls interrupted and Vel looked for two seconds before remembering where he was and yanked his head in the opposite direction, looking morosely at the chapstick on the floor, "I think he's telling the truth."

"Cassidy," Ms. Patton addressed with a coldness that told Vel she was still glaring at him, "He used the oldest excuse in the book. Even if they made it look like it was forced, it was definitely *not.*"

Vel bit the inside of his cheeks. Cassidy Morello was one of those student council types—everyone knew her and her circle of friends was wide and as intricate as her efficiently organized system of color-coded notes. Everyone would probably say she was a nice girl, Vel would even say that, but that's where Vel's notion of her ended. Of course she was nice, what else would she be? At the same time, having her advocate for him like this was a shock and unheard of. There was no way in hell she even knew his name.

"If that's the case," Cassidy deflected with the smoothness of her debate team experience, "he should've at least *looked*."

Vel flinched even though it was true. He just didn't want to be associated with any of this anymore. In case that made him look guilty, though, he morosely corroborated, "I didn't."

"Besides," Cassidy continued, "*Everyone* knows that he's not friends with Mitch Winters."

"God, is anyone?" a second voice complained, standing close to Cassidy "He's such a *jerk*."

Ms. Patton was quiet, clearly chewing through Cassidy's words even though she didn't like it.

"Also, when has, uhh," Cassidy paused, confirming his suspicions.

"Vel," he provided. In the barest of his peripheral vision he saw her nod with recognition.

"When has Vel shown an interest in like, any of this anyway? He just hangs out with Sebbie."

Oh. Well. If looking gay was the frying pan but it got him out of the fire, he wasn't going to complain. And he *certainly* wasn't about to correct her and reveal that he *did* like girls, because that was going to be burning the ladder she was lowering him.

After an agonizingly long deliberation, Ms. Patton finally released his arm and Vel stumbled away, pushing the door further open before slipping out into the hallway. The conversation was continuing as the door swung closed but Vel wasn't about to be around to hear it. Ducking his head low he dashed to the boys' locker room, nearly bowling over some freshmen that were exiting when he flung himself inside. Yanking on his cargo shorts, he realized how hot his face had become. Hot with shame, hot with embarrassment, so hot he couldn't think past the primal urge to clothe himself. Though he usually thought of himself as protecting Sebbie instead of the other way around, this would've never have happened if Sebbie had been here. They might've targeted Sebbie and Vel protecting him would've been enough to stop it. He yanked his backpack out of his locker, slammed it shut, realized he was shaking as he struggled with the padlock, then left. Vel hung back from the main pack of students waiting on the bell, wishing he was ten inches shorter.

"Hey, Vel,"

He startled, looking down to see Cassidy and her friend had approached him.

"Oh. Hey." he said, mouth feeling cottony.

"Sorry about that. I talked with the girls and I think they feel pretty bad too."

"Uh-huh."

"You doing alright?"

He stared at her.

"Where's Sebbie?"

Before he could answer the friend—what was her name? Megan?—next to her widened her eyes and inhaled deep, "Uh, no, don't ask about that."

"Oh," Cassidy said, looking down, "Sorry."

It wasn't her fault, but he had absolutely no idea what to say to that. Still after a moment of awkwardness she brightened up again.

"Hey, have you heard what the school district's doing?"

"No," he said then scrunched his face, "I uh, had a busy weekend."

"They're cutting Mexican-American studies!" Cassidy said. Vel watched in muted interest as she fired up, her brown eyes intense and her feet planted firm. Though it was clear she was only talking to him because of this issue and not what had just happened, he was oddly glad for it. It meant she wasn't dwelling on the embarrassment of his boxers scuttling across the locker room floor. From the fire in her voice he could tell it wasn't feigned either—this was her passion, and certainly *why* she was in student council in the first place, "Can you freaking believe it?! Okay maybe if we were like, I don't know, *Wisconsin* or something, but *Arizona?!*"

"It's *so* dumb," Megan piped in with an eyeroll that seemed so natural it might have just been her drawing a breath.

"They're really doing that?" Vel asked. He had heard rumors, sure, but to Megan's word, it seemed almost *too* dumb to do.

"They're pushing for it!" Cassidy stomped her foot, "My mom and I have been going to school board meetings and they don't give two shits!"

"Damn," Vel said, more because she swore than anything else.

"Vel, you're Mexican, right?"

"Guilty." he replied, then internally winced at the word.

"His last name's *Velasquez*, Cassie!"

"Well *I don't know!*" Cassidy huffed, "He could be, uh, Colombian, or, um—*anyway*, if it goes through we'll be staging a walk-out. You in?"

Vel blinked a few times, taking extra time to process what she was saying. When he did, he nodded slightly, "Yeah. Sure." Anything to skip school, especially if it was going to go on like this. He had the notion that court cases took time, and he had no idea how long he was going to have to suffer school without Dom and Sebbie.

Elated, Cassidy cheered. As soon as she had done so she

turned to Megan, chatting excitedly and meandering away from Vel through the crowd of students. He watched, but he hardly processed anything. There was no room in his head to do so, not even for the proposed walk-out. If things were better he could see himself saying yes regardless, but he also doubted Cassidy would've talked to him personally. He let out a sigh that released no tension. The bell rang and Vel waited a few extra seconds before he followed the pack.

13

None of his other classes were much better. From Mrs. Peterson who played favorites (of which Vel wasn't one) to Mr. Hauser who could smell his missing homework from down the hallway, Vel was alone. Vel was so alone that he curled up at the far corner of the lunch table he usually shared with Dom and Sebbie, eating the shitty squared pizza as the cacophony of students mulled to a white noise. He wished he could say he couldn't wait to go home, but.

The radio was tuned to some Spanish program Vel couldn't keep up with. Tía Gloria was cleaning the kitchen. Vel slipped by without a word. He was sure his tía had seen him, but both by the grace of letting him go *and* a quiet punishment for his insubordination, she ignored him. He was going to hole himself up in his room, wanting to fool himself that he could've done homework. But he knew better—rather he knew that nothing would be off his mind enough to do so.

Instead, he grabbed the cordless phone in the hallway and carried it out the back door along with the phone book propped behind it. There wasn't much of a porch to sit on, just two sun-dried steps of wood that listed heavily when he sat down. The sun was hot but the breeze was already cooling for the coming evening. Crickets chirped while the occasional bird weighed in beneath the sounds of benign domestic squabbles and kids slamming screen doors in the brief hours they had before dinner. When he found it he dialed the non-emergency number for the police department, fumbling his way through asking for Sergeant Kulasiewicz. After a brief hold, her stony voice cut through the dull crackle of the phone.

"Kulasiewicz."

"Sarge. Can I talk to you?" He paused for a moment both terrifying and vulnerable, "About the case."

"About the case, yes." she clarified, sparing no extraneous sympathy even though she must've picked up on his meeker tone. To be frank, he found that fine. Almost preferable. Sarge was allowed to ignore his feelings because she was actually *doing* something about it. Vel took in a shaky breath.

"You know that parking lot the roadrunner took us to?"

He could audibly hear her teeth grit and that gave him the briefest spark of joy. *Yes, Sarge, the roadrunner magic. Remember when the unexplainable happened? Why don't I firmly state that on the line while you have no choice but to humor me because you were there too?*

"Yes." she answered in a way that sounded physically painful.

"Who owns that lot? The theater?"

"It's been abandoned for a while."

"Yeah but does someone own it?" Vel prodded, "Like, a church took over for what, five years? Only?"

"Longer than that," Sarge corrected, "But it didn't last that long, no. Maybe ten years at most."

"That's weird, ain't it?" he had not realized that the smoothness of his voice had returned as he got onto an open train of thought, "Like, my tía's a nun, right. Churches don't pay taxes. Could they not pay the rent? Too small a congregation? What happened there?"

The distant sound of a plane grew louder, blotting out Sarge's words and Vel squinted in irritation at the sky. When its contrails grew puffy and light he asked Sarge to repeat what she had said.

"Potentially. It wasn't a Catholic church."

"Is it worth looking into? I mean. With the tire prints on the body and in the parking lot being similar and all...Maybe the building has some history."

"Hm," Sarge said, not without interest. Vel expected her to shoo him away after thanking him for the nugget of information, helping yet not helping at the same time because he was too young to know anything anyway. But to his surprise (and further, overwhelming gratitude) she added, "Might be a good idea to ask for a record of Green's checkbook."

"For cross-reference!" Vel exclaimed, jumped at his own excitement, then glanced over his shoulder to make sure his tía was still preoccupied, "D'ya think?!"

"Slow down," Sarge chastised, "Nothing's been found yet."

"But if," Vel continued at the same speed, "If Green was looking to purchase the building or maybe the lot off of the owner, and maybe, what if, like, okay—,"

"*Slow down*," Sarge chastised again, "Remember no one thinks thetheater has anything to do with your friends."

"What about you?" Vel asked, sliding his knees close together on the steps. Sarge was quiet as if he had slapped her across the face with such a blunt, innocent question. When it took her longer than he expected to answer he decided to add a backhand, "What do you think?"

"...I think we do not have time for a proper investigation." she answered finally, "You raised a lot of good questions, but we don't have the time to follow them up."

"Why *not*," Vel huffed, anger bubbling up over the fear that boiled it.

"Because—," Sarge started, stopped herself, and then in the silence that followed Vel felt the full weight of what everyone had been putting on him. Whether or not Sarge was in on it seemed to not matter—the choice was made without her and she was clearly just there to see it through. Vel's face hardened as he set his jaw. Once more her silence went longer than he expected, and in an attempt to keep his rage tamped down he pulled out a cigarette and flicked his lighter, all with the phone tucked in his shoulder so Sarge heard everything. Sure he was smoking illegally. Kids did illegal shit all the time. At least it wasn't murder. At least it wasn't spinning the wheel to blame the murder on someone else. At least it wasn't forcing a kid to do the investigation for them on the assumption that it'd flop. Sarge inhaled, likely calming herself down as she answered very lowly, "Because the case is going to trial faster than usual."

"Oh yeah?" Vel spoke through the cigarette in his mouth, clearly mad and snarky because of it, "Fancy that."

"If—you want my opinion," Sarge struggled.

"I want *some* of your opinions." *The rest you can shove up your ass.*

"Your friends are very, very, very lucky they had you investigating."

That was supposed to feel good. He knew it did, somewhere on the edges of the hollowness that was sitting in his chest. It felt really good. But not as good as it should've felt when they were both still behind bars and with little hope to sway the trial.

"Sarge," he said, the smoke making his dry throat low and gruff in a way that he hoped gave him maturity. Credibility.

Anything, "Did you test the grill of Dom's car for blood? The tires?"

"Both came back negative," she confirmed, "And the grill pattern doesn't match what's found on Green's body."

"Isn't that enough?"

She was quiet again. Some two houses down he heard two kids a decade or so younger than him tussling in their dusty lawn. There was a pause, a shout, then the unmistakable musical sound of a ball being kicked. He saw it fly in his peripheral vision, the spinning white hexagonal plates stainedorange from loyal use. Whooping followed as the kids chased its trajectory, unconcerned of any danger whether that was rattler or car. Of course that wasn't to say they weren't careful; they'd shout to each other whenever they saw a car turn down the thin residential road and sequester themselves off to the side. Vel wondered about the grim reality that someone could set those kids up to fail, that *he* could if he really wanted to. He could do something as easy as walking over and offering them a puff of his cigarette. Or he could do something as complex as leading them deeper into the city or worse into the wild Parks around them. It made him shudder. Never in a million years would he ever do such a thing. He would never hurt a kid like that nor allow them to come to harm under his watch. But he *could*.

And if someone wanted to save their own skin badly enough, they could do it to Dom and Sebbie too.

"Sarge. Do you know who's making the trial happen so soon?" he asked, still tense and angry with the weight pushing him down.

She sighed and he was expecting another brick wall to pound his fists against, but to his surprise she actually answered, "His name is Owen Schrute. He lives in the neighborhood of the crime scene and is trying to have it solved quickly so children can play safely in the playground again."

"Oh," Vel said, taking it at face value. He ashed the cigarette on the ground in front of the stairs. Sebbie lived in a fairly well-to-do area, leastways compared to the ones Vel had always resided in. He supposed it made sense that someone who lived nearby had money to throw around as they wanted, "What does he do?"

Sarge answered almost thoughtlessly, which was good for Vel. He had long since caught on that pure information was her forte rather than the nitty gritty emotional stuff *despite* the fact that she tolerated him, "Schrute and Sons Management owns a fair amount of commercial buildings in the Tucson area, mostly entertainment centers."

"You mean like theaters?"

Sarge paused. Again, quiet. Again, children playing over the sounds of both nature and distant traffic. Vel raised his eyebrows and waited.

"So you're gonna look into that, right, Sarge?" he needled.

He heard her shift uncomfortably before she managed a pathetic, "We'll see."

Yeah. You'd better. He put the cigarette back in his lips and took a nice long drag.

He was going to say something on the exhale, all cool and suave like a real P.I. of a dark and gritty noir film. But from inside the house his tía roared and Vel jumped out of his skin, scrambling to his feet and fumbling between the phone and cigarette in his hands.

"Jeró if you are smoking a cigarette by the time I look out the window I am pouring your dinner down the drain!!"

"Shit," he gasped into the receiver, "Gotta go, Sarge, bye,

see you in court!!"

Vel slipped on hanging up the phone and dropped it to the stairs before sprinting away from the house and down the street. Couldn't see him smoking a cigarette if he wasn't actually there to see in the first place, right?

Blowing past the two kids playing soccer, Vel panted through the cig still in his mouth, "Hey, you didn't see me, I didn't go in this direction, right? Cool thanks *bye!*"

"¡¡Jerónimo!!" his tía's voice rang clear across the neighborhood, meaning that she had physically stepped outside. Vel yelped and tore away as fast as his knees and smoked–up lungs would take him.

14

Sarge led him through the Pima County Courthouse. Unlike the police station and the medical examiner's, the courthouse was ornate and grand. Open arches allowed sunlight from the courtyard to rest on the earthy tiles that led into the building proper, with its peach-stone walls reaching to pale seafoam ceilings above from colorful mosaics below. Vel allowed his eyes to wander as a distraction. He had the weekend to cobble together the final project for his history class, and something about the Courthouse might as well be it. What that something was he didn't know, but he'd figure it out.

He had figured it out so far.

Part of him wanted to ask Sarge what he should say on the stand. The other, smarter, more adult part of him knew he'd be fed and fluffed to a police sergeant's liking. With everyone's peripherals knowing that Vel and his friends were being set up, he stayed quiet despite the anxiety in his chest. If everyone knew they were being set up, did anyone know *who* and *why?* Or was it just a feeling in the air without a direction?

He stuck his hands in his pockets as they approached the courtroom, thumbing the affects he had thought to bring. In one pocket there was the bloodsoaked sucker wrapper (now dried a sickly brown) and the paint chipped from the jail bars. In the other, stupidly, there was the toy car he had enchanted. He had initially wanted to bring more, it's not like his shorts didn't have enough pockets, but he held back. The last thing he needed was a bailiff confiscating something *obviously* important like his mother's necklace.

Funny how quickly he now felt naked without her wrapped around his neck.

What he *did* wear was almost nice enough for Church, though not to hear Tía Gloria say it. A nice pale green button down t-shirt was more effort than he put in for school without the stuffiness of his Sunday best—though now in the courthouse he was having second and third thoughts. Self-conscious, he tugged at his collar and tried to hide his shamed grimace. At least Sarge had a uniform!

"Remember," she interrupted his thoughts with sudden firmness, "You're here to provide a witness statement. Not present evidence."

Vel nodded, unsure if he was grateful because he didn't know how to separate the two in his mind. Sarge either didn't sense this unsureness or didn't care because she didn't clarify. Bosman gave a hollow nod to Sarge in acknowledgment that she returned just as hollowly. His eyes glanced up to Vel and he saw a twinge of that conversation from before; the urge, the regret, and the strange seriousness that he still couldn't place. But he nodded to him too, and Vel figured he trusted Bosman to give the trial his best.

People mingled, waiting for court to be in session. Vel, from his relative height above everyone else there, swept his eyes over all of them. Dom's mother was standing in a small half-circle of some of his siblings, constantly bobbing her head because she was swallowing hard to steel herself. Vel struggled with the push and pull of wanting to go over to her and—well, that was the issue. He didn't know, exactly. Giving his condolences felt juvenile if not condescending; he couldn't exactly give them when they applied to him as well, could he? That, and with Dom's siblings around her...Vel sometimes felt out of place with Dom's family. They all knew each other by nickname, their fights felt surface level even if they were serious, and Dom always *had them*. Vel occasionally flirted with the idea that he was accepted like family too—and they did, they treated him like one of their own and fed his garbage disposal stomach in kind. But something kept him severed in a way that felt painful and inexplicable: Even if they did open their doors to him as an honorary member of the family, would that really replace the one he had—the mother he wasn't allowed to remember, the tía that left the convent for him?

Maybe he was flagellating, but before he could make the decision a pair of eyes cemented him to the spot. Not from Dom's mother, but from a woman of a similar age to her. Shorter, stocky, with full arms and short brown fingers curled tight to her sides. Vel blinked quick, shocked at the intensity of her stare, then looked down at his feet. What was she clocking him as? He thought about the way Ms. Patton looked at him in the girls' locker room and a hot wash of shame he couldn't attribute boiled over him. To make matters worse, the woman staring him down wasn't moving nor releasing him from her gaze, and of course no one else was any the wiser. He swallowed, running through every cordial disarming greeting he knew of to try and throw off her suspicion, if only to get some peace right before watching his friends go on trial.

The only release he found was the near-fashionably late arrival of a man dressed in a suit so notably colorful it prompted

Vel to look up after seeing his pant leg. It was a deep burgundy shimmer, wine-red in the light, dark purple in the shadows. Paisley embroidery of similar shimmering color made up for his undershirt, and to top it off he wore a pleasantly spring green tie. Vel thought he looked like a bunch of grapes at best. He was older, with the long sun-scorched skin of his face wrinkling around pudgy padding. Though his hair was thinning he still had combed product through it into a swoop Vel figured had once been quite fashionable in his younger years. He looked around the room much like Vel had, and made a pit stop to Dom's mother to which there was a very awkward introduction. She, after all, had no idea who Owen Schrute was nor why he was there at the trial, since, despite his attire, he introduced himself as *not a lawyer* with a laugh that did not land.

Vel felt his gut start to tangle with confused bitterness. Schrute was the one expediting the case, for the sake of children playing on the playground or *whatever* excuse he was using to urge his friends into jail faster than they could even finish out one semester of senior year. To dig the man's grave deeper, the woman who had been staring him down fixed her gaze on Schrute, and as intense as her gaze was on Vel it was even worse on him.

That gaze was clearly the reason Schrute disengaged with Dom's mother just as awkwardly as he had engaged, approaching the woman with a crooked smile. Vel watched as he made a familiarizing, dramatic sweep of his arm as a greeting gesture and fumbled over the right accent to call her *Seño Green*, his sloppy Spanish a further insult to the already insulted woman.

After another breath of watching the thick tension form between them, Vel felt hit by a truck. Seño Green meant Rita Green meant *she was the goddamn widow.* And if the widow had been sold on the idea that a couple of rowdy teenagers had thoughtlessly killed her husband, even if by accident, well. Certainly Vel *should* be under her scrutiny then. Much as he'd love to deny it.

Every attempt at cordiality from Schrute bounced off of Rita. It was clear to Vel that they knew each other, but it was hard to tell what their previous relationship was. Whatever it had been, Schrute seemed to try to put that aside for the sake of the trial—even though he didn't even *mention* the trial, something Vel was struggling to understand if that offended him or not. After all, shouldn't he *care* that he was here, shouldn't he care that he was there to bear witness to two teenagers being tried for manslaughter at best? Manslaughter they didn't commit? That it seemingly wasn't a thought in the man's head made fury brew in Vel's skin. He bit his lip, knowing he had to calm down.

Then Schrute produced a candied sucker of the same black cherry flavor found at both the park and the theater. Now, if he lived in one place and owned another, perhaps it didn't warrant high conspiracy. But watching Rita's expression disintegrate into resignation as she took the sucker made Vel teeter on the edge his wiser subconscious was trying to keep him away from. Rita sighed, relaxing tension from her shoulders as the sucker unwrapped and went straight into her mouth for the mildest comfort.

Now, what did *that* all mean? Vel found himself staring at her just as hard as she stared at him when out of nowhere Sebbie's parents appeared in front of him.

Clapping his hands over his mouth did nothing to stifle the yelp, further emasculating him. Mrs. Moore's delicate hands were clawed into her elbows, just as she always was.

"Mr. Velasquez," she addressed humorlessly, "Do you have any interest in this case?"

"Jeez," Vel gasped, "Of course I do! Sebbie's my—,"

"*Why?*" she cut in, and Vel felt a pang of indignant anger.

"I was *saying*, Sebbie's my friend. Dom too! I wanna—,"

"Do you have anything to do with the case?"

"I mean," Vel began, frustrated and unable to think quick enough to know if telling her the whole truth would be a good idea or not, "Yeah, I want to—,"

"*How?*"

"Jesus Christ!" Vel broke. He had had fights with his tía where they overlapped each other, but they had only ever layered their yells in their impressive stubbornness to not be cut off. Never, even with her, had he felt this steamrolled, "Do you want me to answer your questions or not?!"

She narrowed her eyes. Vel felt a pang of panic. Not every parent was his tía and would not respond well to his insolence.

"I mean," Vel tried to regain, "I'm just uh, nervous. Character witness, y'know."

Mrs. Moore didn't seem convinced, but more than that she seemed unconvinced in the way that pricked the back of Vel's neck. There was something she wasn't divulging, something she had been searching for just by speaking to him alone. Vel felt his walls close in tight, protecting whatever it is she wanted to know away from her. She had no real power over Vel and couldn't pry it out of him nor would that knowledge damage him in any way.

Sebbie, on the other hand.

She tightened her jaw, straightened herself, then turned away. For a brief moment her husband's equally withering stare lingered on Vel, and he returned it with a hollowness he hoped was uninterpretable.

When the tension sank back into the milling curiosity it had been before, Vel deflated against the wall. It was no secret that the Moores did not like him, but as the dust settled there was a frantic fear that was taking hold in Vel's chest as he realized just how *much* they did not like him. Had it always been like this? He remembered Sebbie talking about how his parents don't listen to him in relatability to how Vel's tía also didn't listen, though in a different way. At one point Sebbie said to him that he was giving up trying, in a defeatist tone that betrayed all the shame he felt. Vel didn't have an argument for or against it at the time, but he was forming one now: If Sebbie had protected him from the specifics of what his parents had said because of something deeper and much more frightening than simply not getting along with them, then...Then Vel could not blame him.

He didn't blame him before, but now he was *afraid*, and now he wanted Sebbie away from his parents not just for his friend's sake but for his.

Vel rubbed his chest, feeling the rapid beat of his heart. There was a harrowing surrealism to how *real* it was. He thought of the last time he saw Sebbie, the long glance he gave him after he insinuated that he was using magic to help his case. And, he would never, Sebbie would never, Sebbie loved him, they were best friends, and Vel loved him too. Maybe that was the issue. Not that Vel could stop, but he didn't know if the problem lied with Sebbie or with his parents or with Vel, himself—or if magic would *make* Vel the problem.

Taking in a breath, Vel held it, then released. Midway through his release another person appeared in front of him and he yelped. Again.

Rita Green stared him down just as intensely as Mrs. Moore,

but this close he finally saw that it was a more outright sorrow he couldn't place. Stifling a string of swear words, Vel stammered, "Wh-what do *you* want?!"

"You," she said, her voice comfortable in English with the audible foundation of a Spanish accent underneath, "You're a witness?"

"I'm, uh," he fumbled, repeating what he had told Mrs. Moore with the same mumbling cadence, "Y'know. Character witness."

Rita Green did not say anything, just continued to stare at him. Vel watched her, unsure of what to say or do when he was still frazzled from the Moores' interrogation. After a while the corner of her lip curled into a frown.

"I-I don't think," he chanced a glance at Sarge, "I mean. I don't think they did it, Mrs. Green."

She looked hurt. He wondered about the annoyance she displayed in front of Owen Schrute and the resignation of the black cherry sucker he had offered her. Rita swallowed something in her throat—a widow's regret, perhaps—and said, "I'm sorry." It was entirely unclear what outcome she expected or even wanted for the death of her husband. It was also unclear what Vel was supposed to feel.

One thing that was clear was the relief when the court allowed everyone inside; relief that was horribly brief since the reality bore down on him like the desert sun. When the call to rise came Vel felt hollow and giddy and anxious and angry all at once.

Sebbie and Dom sat in the defendants' chairs, the backs of their heads visible, their posture bent with insecurity and anticipation. Vel wished this had been a classroom, where he could pass notes or throw paper balls to get their attentionTo have them look back at him again.

But it wasn't. And there was nothing he could do about it.

Sarge went up to the stand to deliver the facts as stonily as ever, minus what they had found at the theater parking lot. Vel agitated. Bosman went next, corroborating Sarge's findings while providing that the markings on Green's body were most likely caused by a sedan. When questioned he admitted that it was hard to determine the make and model, though by measurements alone it couldn't have been as big and heavy as a minivan. There was a tartness to Bosman's voice, an annoyance to be there, annoyance at the short investigation, annoyance that this went to court at all. Annoyance, and when he caught his eye for the briefest of moments, Vel saw bitter apology.

He was in a strange limbo—observing, hearing words, knowing his time was soon but being unable to predict when. Sitting in between the silent judgments of all in attendance, whether that was for his friends' favor or against. Or whether or not they were just here to see the outcome of it all anyway. With such a grisly crime happening near the playground, why wouldn't they? They were thinking of the children. Everyone was thinking of the children.

Sebbie and Dom didn't count.

"The defense would like to call Jerónimo Velasquez to the stand."

Vel blundered, standing only when they called him the second time. Tripping over his own feet, he blubbered "Yes, your honor," as he pawed his way to the well. It was hard to tell what the judge was thinking in all of this. At least, not until his eyes flicked down and he drew a breath.

"Mr. Velasquez, are you alright to take the stand?"

"Uh," he stammered, "Just nervous, your honor."

He raised both his bushy eyebrows, increasing Vel's confusion. Then, from the defense's table, he heard Sebbie gasp.

"*Vel,*"

"Wh," he sputtered, seeing more and more of the court's eyes on him. More. Concern and shock rose high on their faces and Bosman sprang to his feet. That's when he felt a warmth spread on the face of his right thigh. Horror swamped him, and when he looked down the relief that it wasn't piss was not strong enough to overcome the visceral fear of blood. Vel placed a hand on his pants, drawing it back with a gleaming red smear from the soaked fabric that stupefied him stiff.

"A recess, your honor, goddammit!" Bosman snapped as he barged into the well. Vel staggered when Bosman clamped on his arms to drag him to the door, "You alright, kid? You feel faint?"

"A-A little dizzy," Vel said, dazed and giving the most incorrect tone for the amount of blood staining his shorts. Bosman swore and hurried him out into the hallway. When Vel followed up with a pathetic, "It's just nerves, I think," Bosman swore again.

"*Nerves?!*"

"I don't think—," his shoulder crumpled against the bathroom door without apology as Bosman pushed him to the far wall, "I don't think it's my blood."

"*What,*" Bosman barked as he put a hand calloused by latex and chemicals to Vel's forehead. Then his cheek, smearing away a thin layer of sweat from his skin, "You talked crazy in my lab, but that's downright horseshit loopy, you know that?"

Vel raised his bloodstained hand, "I don't feel any pain, is all."

"Do you know how *bad* that sounds? All the blood draining from the area of a *femoral* artery and you don't feel any goddamn thing?!" he stepped back to assess what he could see of the wound, but his hands hovered away from touching anything that could've been hurt. Vel folded his hand over the sticky blood drying on his palm and reached down.

"I'm serious, I think...I think I'm okay," he carefully rolled up the bloody pant leg to expose the unbroken—if reddened—skin of his thigh, "...See?"

Bosman scowled but knelt down despite himself. After a moment of peering with no result, he glanced up at Vel, "Can I poke and prod?"

Vel nodded, trusting Bosman for reasons he couldn't parse as the older man gently investigated. No pain, no wound; nothing but red smeared on his fingertips. In disbelief, Bosman gingerly sniffed his hand to confirm it was, indeed, blood. Vel watched his face go from open caution to something far more reserved and protected. *Witch*, Vel's mind yelped. *Brujo.* Bosman let out a pained noise as he helped himself back up to his feet, avoiding

Vel's eyes until he directly addressed him.

"I would say that's a helluva nosebleed, but I saw the stain grow outward from your leg. What's in your pocket?"

"Nothing much," Vel said, digging a hand in, "Just, uh, trash, really."

Bosman twisted his mouth skeptically, but when Vel produced nothing more than a sopping wet wrapper that, even if the sucker had been made with only blood, could not have been enough to soak through his pants. Vel tried to smooth it out, shaking out blood that spattered on the floor. One saturated corner tore off and he struggled to pull the wrapper back up into the cradle of his palm.

"Uh. You're gonna have to explain that one, kid."

"I got this one at the theater parking lot I went to with Sarge. Another one just like it was at the crime scene. It did it once before not too long ago," Vel said, "Or I mean, that's when it first got soaked in blood."

He glanced at Bosman and the utter blankness on his face told him everything he needed to know. Carefully, he unwrapped his thoughts one by one.

"I don't know how to explain how it happened, but I put one wrapper on the crime scene and the other at the theater. The crime scene one stayed dry, but the one at the theater...Well it was more the uh, thing I used to represent the victim, that started pooling blood on the floor. Uncontrollably. And this was the wrapper that got soaked in it. And today, I guess when people started talking, it...It—doesn't matter. It just freaked out and started bleeding in my pocket."

Bosman was dead silent. Vel searched his expression for anything to understand. Twisting his mouth, he came to the decision he'd have to lead him on his train of thought in order to keep him on his side.

"Bosman I don't think...It's more than my friends not killing Green. I don't think he was killed at that park at all. I think it happened miles away, at the abandoned theater that Schrute owns. My friends and I drive past that park every Saturday, that's true. If someone knew that, it'd be easy to blame us for an accident, easier still because we're young and dumb and don't know shit, right, Doc? And if...well, if a murder or a dead body wound up on property that you needed to sell or buy and you panicked...," He held his breath. He was, after all, talking to a medical examiner with a doctorate and years of experience in pathology. The urge to argue with Vel was distorting his features, but the fact that he had watched a dead body have an allergic reaction kept that urge at bay. Though he hadn't referenced it directly, Bosman *had* used the evidence drawn from that very reaction in his testimony moments earlier.

It would've been easy to dismiss Vel. It would've also been disingenuous.

The next minutes hung in the balance as they judged each other.

"...Damn kids," Bosman muttered, "Finding a way to make my gut feel two things at once."

"Good enough for me. That's how I feel a lot of the time anyway." Vel responded quietly.

"Oh yeah?" Bosman grunted, "And how do you decide which one to listen to?"

Vel shrugged as his answer. Bosman scoffed, hints of amusement coloring the corners of his mouth.

"Still, that's...," Bosman searched for words that never came, then finally settled with, "...a lot of blood."

"How much?" Vel asked.

Bosman's face curled like he was about to say *too goddamn much* with all the pathologicalmeasurements to back him up when the door swung open. Both of them looked over to see Schrute pause.

"Is the kid alright?" he asked, too clumsy to be warm about it. At the same time Vel was oddly relieved to be called a *kid* after everything. But he was still suspicious as to why *he* was the one to come check up on him.

"I'm fine," he responded, terse enough for Bosman to glance back. Whatever calculations he ran he ran quick, and Vel noticed he squared his shoulders just a little. Though Bosman was calmer than he would've liked, as though he was toeing the line between being on Vel's side and the other adult's.

"Just a burst blood blister," Bosman lied, "Should be good to go soon enough."

Schrute nodded, then, as if struck with remembering where he was and why, he fumbled with his zipper before turning to the urinal. Vel gave a small exasperated huff and started wiping the blood away with thin paper towels.

"So you're," Schrute continued, staring at Vel while a stream of piss hit the ceramic, "Their friend, right? One of those boys?"

"Yeah." Vel answered, cringed, then said, "Can you, uh, focus on the fact you're pissing?"

This request seemed to fly way over Schrute's head, because he *kept talking*, "I don't like seeing boys all locked up like that, I'm sorry."

"What's it to you?" Vel snapped, unable to contain himself once the smallest bit of pressure finally released, "You wanted this to go to court, right?"

"Well, I," Schrute pulled his words together to answer, "I wanted it resolved quickly, yes. It'll put them back in school sooner, would make parents less—,"

"You *rushed* the investigation!" Vel accused. Bosman pushed his shoulder into Vel, discreetly stopping his tirade before it spiraled out of control. Though Vel quietly obeyed, it did nothing to douse the fury building inside him. It was readable in his eyes, and he had no pretenses about that.

Schrute paused, his stream weakening in tandem. It was as if he had not even seriously considered what Vel had said to be a consequence. If at all, it was surely a *necessary* one; the terror Vel and his friends felt couldn't have been anything but surmountable, especially if they were innocent. Something akin to hesitation entered Schrute's voice as he responded, "You...have to understand. When I woke up that morning and saw a body mangled outside my home, I—,"

"So you didn't see it happen?! Why frame Dom then?!"

Bosman put a hand on his arm, no longer discreet.

Schrute patiently provided, "He drives by my home all the time—,"

"So do I!" Vel snapped, "Wanna put me on the chopping block too?!"

"Vel," Bosman finally said, and the fact that he remembered and used his name made him stop. Not without rage, as Bosman's attitude exuded nothing but defeatism to him. They were in court, it was too late. The damage was already being done. Scoffing, Vel tossed the crumpled towels thick with blood in the waste basket. Maneuvering out from behind Bosman, Vel took one last shot at Schrute.

"Great job thinking of the kids."

Zipping up, Schrute opened his mouth to respond but Vel had had enough and shouldered his way past him. He had done so roughly enough that it was borderline petulant, and from incredulity over that petulance Schrute missed that Vel had slipped something into his pocket.

16

"And you, Mr. Velasquez? How do you drive?"

Vel put his tongue in his cheek to think. The stand was both better and worse than giving a presentation at school. Better, because it felt worthwhile to even be there in the first place. Better because he had genuine conviction over what he was saying. Worse, because, well.

Court had resettled with tension that had its focal point set on him. The general unease from the inexplicability of what had happened hardened that tension, which did not help the fact that with each subsequent testimony and hiccup it was becoming increasingly clear that the case was an unholy mess. From the rushed—therefore botched, not even because of Vel's interference—investigation to all evidence leaning hard on hearsay at best, the case had made the judge agitated that they were there at all. Pair it with Vel's sudden stigmata (it wasn't, but it'd piss his tía off to call it that, so call it that he did) and the tension had turned from annoyed to spooked.

All eyes were on him not just because he was on the stand, in other words. Interestingly though, out of all the eyes from Sebbie to Sarge, the ones he felt the most were those of Rita Green. She was direly invested in his every word as he described his friends' behavior and the likelihood of their recklessness.

Lack thereof, rather. She shifted in her seat whenever the attorney changed the topic, as if she wanted to tell him to stop, go back, keep talking. But all he was talking about were the mundane ways he spent his teenage afternoons with his friends. It was peculiar. He couldn't place why.

Her scrutiny was welcome, if nothing else. If Rita didn't believe his friends did it, and if Sarge didn't have enough evidence and Bosman presented reasonable doubt and his character witness supported all that—then. Then they'd have no choice but to let his friends go.

Still his heart raced. He had planted a failsafe in Schrute's pocket, if it worked the way he wanted it to. Something to give Schrute pause, something to make him think twice before roping kids into a scandal out of overblown concern for a neighborhood that didn't need any. Vel drew in a breath then held it, calming down. The rest of his testimony was going to go easier.

Until Rita started coughing. It was innocent enough; she sounded like she had swallowed saliva down the wrong pipe. Vel paused in answering the attorney to wait for it to clear, but when it didn't Schrute dug his hand into his pocket and drew out a wad of tissues. Vel's heart spiked again, this time in frustration. The paint chip wrapped in bathroom tissue he had slipped into his pocket could very well—was most certainly—wadded up with the rest of them. He watched as Rita took the tissues without looking and he jerked, tempted for a split second to stop her.

But that would've been ridiculous, and on top of that would've revealed he had done something to Schrute. Regaining himself before it became suspicious, Vel slumped back into his seat. Well. So much for the failsafe. So much for his personal justice. If that was punishment for trying to bend magic to his will, then—whatever, he'd complain about it later.

Later would not come, however. Or perhaps it came too soon. Rita stood up out of common courtesy, aiming to leave for the restrooms. Vel watched as she held the bundle of tissues-plus-paint-chip to her mouth and coughed.

Then he watched the skin on her forehead flatten out as soon as she had stepped past Schrute. It was sudden, startling, and pushed Rita back down the aisle until her back hit something hard but invisible.

All eyes were suddenly not on him.

Rita, stunned, flailed her arms out like she was blind, mapping out an invisible enclosure that had captured her. Vel's hands gripped the edges of the stand. As murmurs of confusion heightened, he calculated where her arms stopped, skin flattening and whitening against surfaces no one could see. It was a box. A relatively small one, one that would squash him if kept in for too long, and he knew it too. The dimensions of the box were six-foot-by-nine, a small holding cell just like his had been.

Vel felt himself grow cold and quiet as the confusion burst into alarm. Schrute moved freely from within the cell that trapped Rita. She began to bang on the walls, the echoes metal and hollow as prison bars. The bailiff sprang forward, gently grabbing Rita by the arm to try and lead her out of whatever hysteria had gripped her only to find that she could not move anywhere he tried to lead her. What was firstly thought as hysteria turned to real panic, not stayed even by the gavel.

"What is this," the judge demanded, "What is going on? Mrs. Green?"

"I'm trapped!" she yelled, desperately clawing at the unseen bars that made frantic, terrifying music in her stead, "Something's trapping me, I can't move!"

Vel had risen halfway from his seat, viciously caught between leaping to her aid and how doing that would reveal the whole fucked gambit. In the sudden wave of bodies and arms moving to either help Rita or get far away from her in case she was somehow contagious, a pair of eyes settled back on him again. Vel met Sarge's glance. Whatever was on his face certainly convinced her that he knew *something* of what was going on, and furthermore that must've told her that he also had *no* idea what to do.

Then one other pair of eyes settled on Vel, and he swallowed hard and turned to meet Sebbie. He didn't know what to do.

Rita's banging became a frenzied cacophony, beating beneath her screams for release, "Let me out!! *Let me out!!! I didn't do it, let me out!!*"

Distressed, Vel finally started clambering out of the stand proper to try and pull her from the enchantment as her words filled the courtroom.

"It was him!! It was *him!!*" Rita screamed, and Vel *knew* that already, that's why he set the trap in Schrute's pocket, not hers, it was Schrute, he had done it, he had—, "*He* wanted to buy the theater when he *knew* our finances were low! He *knew* our son couldn't afford rent! He *knew* we had promised to help him no matter what happened! And he wanted to *buy the theater!!*"

Vel had made it to Sarge's side when he stopped, furrowing his brow in confusion. This earned him another glance from her, this time with both their wheels turning in tandem, and they looked back to Rita.

"He *knew* we had barely managed to keep our home! He knew, he knew, he *knew!!* But he wanted it, he wanted his visionary exotic gardens, he wanted something *we could not have!!!* And

I, our son, our *son*,"

Suddenly Rita slammed her hands on the invisible bars and curled her fingers tight around them, dragging her nails down the metal in a screeching noise that seized his heart before she devoured it, staring at him, staring at him once again *so intensely* with such angry sorrow that Vel suddenly found himself afraid.

"And *you. You!!!*"

Oh fuck, did she know?

"You weren't supposed to *be* there!" Rita howled at Vel, then her eyes darted to Sebbie, then Dom, "*None of you were supposed to be there!!!*"

The court, whoever was left, fell silent. Rita collapsed into her hands and started sobbing. Vel watched the middle-aged woman crumble, forgetting he was there, forgetting he had a body at all. That...This wasn't what he wanted.

"Well, hell," Bosman breathed, "I guess this wasn't a waste of time after all."

Vel couldn't bear to tear his eyes away. This wasn't what he wanted at all. This didn't feel like justice. It was the *truth*, but this couldn't have been justice.

Yet Vel kept quiet as the court struggled to restructure itself, the judge dismissing his friends of all charges as the bailiff continued to try and figure out what to do with Rita. On Vel's money, by the time the tissues dried out from her saliva the walls would fall. But he kept quiet. Kept his mouth shut, and left the courtroom to meet his friends on the other side.

The courthouse seemed normal from the outside, if only because everyone else was oblivious to what had just happened. Vel almost wanted to grab the calm passersby, yell at them, because how could they not know what had just happened?! That Rita Green had become trapped for all to see, that she had become so panicked she had confessed her guilt, she had done it, how could she have possibly have done it? How could she have been harboring a secret like that? How could she have stayed silent when that secret engulfed him and his friends when their youth was all she cared about? Vel knew she felt guilty about that, could feel it in her sorrowed scrutiny. How could she? *Why?* Why did this happen?

It wasn't fair.

Sarge had found him easily once she had determined that the logistics were all in their proper place. Vel had vaguely heard her stony voice cut through the panic as she gathered what had happened. Rita Green had run over her husband in the parking lot of the theater he was on the brink of purchasing from Schrute. It had been a slow collapse over months, losing her patience with him as he sought to cement a fantasy in the wake of the recession. Buy a theater, turn it into a greenhouse— while one son laid off and the other floundering in college.

In the immediate aftermath she could only think to pin the blame on Schrute, but her haste was sloppy and Schrute far too quick on the draw for finding someone else to take the fall. Vel *understood* all of this on a surface level, but at the same time he wondered if he simply just wasn't mature enough to *really* understand. Sure, Rita was driven to the point of murder for the sake of her sons' livelihoods. Got it. Understandable.

But *why*, though? Look at what Rita had done to his friends, done to herself! What about her sons?

Sarge took place beside him at a distance just enough that they could speak but far enough that she didn't play into any pretenses of cordiality. At least she remained the same, despite everything. At least he had that.

The silence set in, the quiet murmur of the courthouse while shadows shifted back and forth in the sunset light. Waiting for his friends brought a sort of liminality to the area, the assuredness of his success with the blunt knowledge that things would not be the same for a very long time. Never, actually, because in months they would all graduate and then life would begin anew and to think it all started here waiting for them to be released. Waiting for the paperwork to be finished and filed. He was happy. He thought so, anyway. But Sarge picked beneath the surface.

"So. You did it. Your friends walk free."

"...Yeah."

"And you're not happy about this?"

"I am. I will be, I think."

"What's holding you back?" she asked, dry. After all, he had been so full of such brazen energy that he should've been bouncing off the walls. He had gotten what he wanted. This was what he had wanted—consequences and all.

"It's not...fair," he pushed out, not understanding why it was so frustrating to say, "It doesn't feel fair."

"It is." Sarge responded, not so firm that it felt like she was arguing with him, but firm enough that he knew she would not waver from that belief. A wash of aghast disbelief hit him and his throat hurt swallowing down the burst of emotion he wanted to barrage her with.

"No it isn't," Vel spat, "It's not. It's not fair, why do you think I care so much?"

"You're young," she answered, flatly and quickly enough that it felt like she expected him to say that. Vel scoffed. Funnily enough it didn't feel premature to do so, and even more than that it didn't feel immature either. Something righteous started to burn in his chest, different than the fervor he initially set out with. Surely Sarge understood that.

Well, surely Sarge, as a police sergeant, as a law enforcement official, should've understood that the world just wasn't fair on the most basic levels. If it was fair, murder wouldn't be a thing, right? Yet here she was.

"*Ugh*," Vel dismissed, intentionally petty to over-prove her point, "Fine. Catch you in ten years." If she didn't see it his way now, maybe she would in the future. With the strange aptitude he found himself having in aiding the investigation, she may even suffer the fact that he'd be around to nag her about it too.

Stranger still, it wasn't the thought of sticking around to annoy Sarge that felt uplifting. No, it was that he had *any* aptitude at all. That he held some talent, that it was Dom the writer, Sebbie the artist, and now Vel the investigator. It sounded so pretentious with his cracked voice and knee braces, but it was something. He could be something, beyond his tía and the choir and his failures in school and the death of his mother and—all of that. He could be Vel because he chose that name for himself. He could be an investigator because he wanted to, and could choose that too.

He heard it then. Something like the lucent church bells his tía always alluded to, brought to him by the familiar shuffling of two sets of feet down a hard hallway. Vel bloomed, shedding all the complications from before. As his friends had always done for him. Roses growing from slurs, a place to cup the real world in their hands as they vented about its rules and cruelties. The quiet muffle of the courthouse exploded into loud whoops of laughter. Three boys stamped their feet as they jumped and tackled into each other, roughhousing like dogs long separated. Howls of *you did it, you made it, I told you, rat halfling bastard c'mere!!* broke into their laughter. Vel's chest hurt from the power of his voice, hurt so much and so deeply he felt like he could cry right then and there. Dom held him tight. Sebbie all but jumped into his arms. For the first time since this started he felt the warmth and comfort as if he was sitting on Dom's couch squashed between the two, belly full of trash and riffing on movies even trashier.

Fatty, Cripple Kid, and The Fag reunited.

"See? You see Dom? My methods *always* work *perfectly!*" Vel arrogantly declared, to the dismissive eyeroll (and relieved smirk) from the dungeon master.

"Keep telling yourself that when it's all just in a dice roll, dude,"

"*Can't* believe you're saying that to my face, standing here after all that!" Vel cried indignantly, giving Dom a gentle punch in the arm.

"Well, we don't know what you even did!" Sebbie interjected, punching them both in the stomach—their height making them easier targets. Vel feigned being hit far harder than Sebbie would ever do, laughing as his friend continued, "You gotta tell us—*prove* it to us, tell us *everything*."

"Alright—," Vel agreed, throwing his hands up in surrender. Then when there was a pause in the punches he pulled Sebbie into his arms so tightly he couldn't move. Soon his shorter legs were kicking in the air and Vel's peals of laughter heightened as he swung him around, "I'll regale an epic tale to the party bard as soon as he's good and tenderized!"

Sebbie laughed alongside him, gripping hard instead of struggling. There was a comeback on his tongue, Vel could feel it, but before it could snap back at him the stern, cold calling of Sebbie's full name cut through their joy and the boy in question tensed like a handful of needles. His grip turned to a push, and he frantically disengaged from Vel until he was several paces away. Both Vel and Dom looked, seeing Sebbie's parents glaring daggers into the center of their friend group. Dom stepped forward, better liked between him and Vel. Still Vel stood up straight and swallowed, his voice deferring and trying to diffuse.

"Just happy to see him, Mr. and Mrs. Moore."

They looked furious, but did not say a word. Sebbie, with his tail tucked between his legs, hurried to their sides. He managed to throw one glance over his shoulder, his eyes promising that he'd see them in school. Otherwise, he all but pretended they didn't exist as his parents escorted him out of the courthouse.

"Goddammit," Vel cussed, "I fucked up, didn't I, Dom,"

"I don't think so," Dom said firmly, "...I guess we'll see."

"They really really think Sebbie and I are gay for each other at school," Vel said, not in panic nor condemnation but caution.

"They think we're *all* gay," Dom reminded him. And that was true in a sense, but there was a difference between hurling gay as a trite insult and accusing it as means to threaten.

"I just—what if, what if his parents think,"

Dom didn't answer for a while. When that time was up, he sighed and put a hand on Vel's shoulder.

"Well. Couple of months and he's eighteen. Right?"

"...Sure." Vel said, more uneasy than frustrated that joy was so unceremoniously stolen from all three of them.

18

Neither of his friends really came back from their imprisonment the same, but something truly haunted Sebbie. Vel noticed the subtler ways Sebbie drew in his limbs to not be in the realm of suggesting that they could've brushed knees.

Normally this wouldn't have been that big of a deal, but Sebbie had withdrawn so far as to not speak to Vel either. Even on days where Vel stuck behind to wait after school, watching Sebbie kick his legs as he had done numerous times before he was silent. Alone, alone in the shadow of the building that was gradually emptying out of everyone except extra curricular students. Alone even though Vel was there. At least until his mother arrived to pick him up; Vel had gotten the timing down just right so that he'd duck away before he'd be seen.

If nothing else Sebbie never sent him away prior to that.

Still, this behavior became blood in the water with bullies sniffing out Sebbie's pain through Vel's concern for him. That concern became a locus of torment, how gay, how wimpy it was for him to *care*. Maybe the gym lockers were never as dangerous as they were when he was alone, but the two of them together garnered a different threat. It was hard to shake. Hard not to look over his shoulder. Hard to pull away.

Vel kept replaying the moments after their release in his

mind; the bright elation from his friend as he pulled him close, no different, no less free than when Sebbie clambered into his car. The very second his parents rounded the corner it was like being doused in ice water. Whatever had happened next behind closed doors was a mystery to Vel—one that didn't necessitate solving. No, solving it would mean a categorical, definitive solution to the problem of Sebbie's behavior—something his parents already did to him. After the less than satisfying conclusion of solving the mystery of Max Green's murder Vel had no desire to become another controlling vice in Sebbie's life, nor did he want to know his deepest darkest secrets. Look how much it already hurt.

But he did want *him* to know that, all of that. Know that Vel was thinking of the situation in this way, calculating the safest passages. That Vel was putting his feet down as firmly as he could on the grounds of respect. How to say that, he didn't know. Too passionate and he'd fall into the trappings where Sebbie could reject him for being too forward, too blunt and it could break the sudden fragility in his friend that now existed outside of his home's walls instead of remaining within.

So there he stayed in the quiet shadows, alone together after school. Waiting for anything. For the day to end, for Sebbie's mother to round the corner. For Vel to sniff and pull out a cigarette two steps too close to Sebbie but not willing to go farther to stretch his guard too thin. For the school year to end, for the days to turn over so Sebbie would be eighteen and start affirming independence in life, for winter to pull back into spring. Waiting for the life they knew to end so the new one could begin, waiting for a day where they didn't have to wait anymore. For the holiday break, for dinner, for homework to be done. For Vel to snuff out his cigarette and bid Sebbie cheers before slinking away to his car. For Sebbie's bright eyes to sink in the back of his neck as he left.

"I don't know." the silence of their waiting broke and Vel startled, nearly dropping his cigarette. He had lost count of how many days had gone by like this. Couldn't have been more than a month. Couldn't have been less than two weeks. Sebbie's voice was soft around the edges as if sandpaper had rendered him rough without blowing the sawdust away, timid and vulnerable yet shaking with the need to speak, "I don't know why I drew a jackrabbit that day."

Vel stared at him, his shock hiding his relief that he was speaking at all. Sebbie had pulled up his hood over his balding head, the fabric worn with years of use and thus must've been comfortable to feel in the chilly air.

"I don't know why I draw things, y'know. Dunno. I just saw you that day and thought you needed cheering up. An' that I could help, maybe," Sebbie gave a withdrawn sigh, then deflated with, "I dunno."

"You did," Vel affirmed gently. Sebbie nodded without a smile, and he saw his eyes contort with a different kind of brightness.

"I'm gonna get out of here, Vel." Sebbie said, "I can't take it anymore."

"Does Dom know?" Vel asked, not surprised in the slightest.

Sebbie shook his head, "Can't risk it. I just gotta go. Got a duffel bag all ready."

Vel took a thoughtful drag and said, "I could swing you to Phoenix and be back in time for whatever. Just let me know. You got a Walkman?"

"Not bringing it," Sebbie said, "Not worth the space,"

"Well, you better work on getting one, because I can't have

American Idiot taking up space in my car forever, y'know."

At that Sebbie pulled a smirk, nodding again before pressing his sleeves to his eyes.

"I don't wanna go," Sebbie confessed in a whisper.

"I don't want you to go, either," Vel said, "But I think you gotta."

"Right," Sebbie choked, "Thanks, Vel."

The sincerity of his gratitude constricted his chest so tightly it sprung tears to Vel's as well. All of his tía's convictions and the beautiful poetry passed down through the Church had not hit him the way hearing the desperation in Sebbie's voice hit him. He hadn't lied to him. He really, really, really didn't want to see him go. Part of him that had a grasp on maturity wondered if he was simply not ready to let go. The other part had a stubborn grasp on the fact that he loved him too much to feel otherwise, whatever that truly meant. Through that, the wish for Sebbie's freedom never felt stronger nor more painful.

"Anytime," Vel said, "I mean it."

"I know you do." Sebbie replied, then glanced down the road, "She'll probably be here in a few minutes."

"Got a plan for when you're gonna jet?"

"Sometime over break."

"Sounds good," Vel said, hanging on the edge of asking *when, how, where,* so he could be there to help. But the time was ticking to a close around them, evidenced by how Sebbie seemed to retreat back into the silence that had plagued him since court. Swallowing any other conversation he wanted to have, Vel reiterated, "Sounds good, Sebbie." then ducked away from sight.

* * *

The sensation was both cool and warm. Wet and stuck. Vel awoke, groggily pawing at the discomfort all over his torso. As his senses gradually followed his consciousness, he pulled at his wet t-shirt to peel it off the skin it was stuck to. Why was it stuck? What was wet? Fumbling in the dark, he flicked his bedside lamp on.

His eyes widened and a scream caught in his throat before it was released. Blood. Thick, dark, and sticky. Frantically Vel kicked his covers off and looked down. Blood pooled in several different places from his collar down to his hips. Terrified and breaths shrill, Vel pressed his hands to his chest and winced at the throbbing pain. It was deep, but not too deep, he thought, he hoped, he pulled his shirt up.

Gasping, he watched his stomach inflate and suck back in, gleaming ruby-red. Arrowheads from his collection slid and fell from wounds in his flesh. His lip quivered in horror, wanting to cry out for his *tía* or his mother or *someone* to come over and explain what had happened. He had been sleeping. The arrowheads had been in their box. How they had gotten into the bed with him wasn't the real mystery but how they had *pierced* him, as though thrust through, he couldn't figure nor fathom. Vel's breaths wheezed and he felt dizzy with confusion. Who had shot him with arrows? What had made it look like he had been tied to a tree and shot just like Saint—

Sebbie.

On a dime his panic turned. Tugging his legs out of the blankets he sprang to his feet. The arrowheads clattered against each other into the bloodstained sheets. He slipped haphazardly into his sandals and opened the front door. With the door halfway open he clambered for the brick cell phone that stayed on the bookcase for his *tía's* use. At the end of the footpath where it connected to the sidewalk a roadrunner stopped and looked at him, eyes gleaming in the low light. He had to get to Sebbie. He *had* to get to Sebbie.

"Help," he tripped over the weather stripping, catching himself on the door frame, "*Help*. If you saw something *help me*," he pleaded, desperate. In the low light the roadrunner's tail twitched. Then it turned to cross the street and Vel skipped over the porch steps to follow it. Soon he was running, his feet hitting pavement that was suddenly not in his neighborhood, nor the next. He couldn't tell if his chest hurt because he was a smoker, or it was the running, or it was the terror. With the cooling early winter air whipping around him, the roadrunner led him across town. The blood further cooled his skin and it made him panic more.

Maybe it had been an open secret at school, but *secret* was the operative word. The first hour after the trial played over and over in Vel's mind, the panic, the righteous urge to pull Sebbie aside, argue with his parents, try to cover him up, try to shut the closet door, but it was a door that couldn't be shut again. He saw the deadening fear on Sebbie's face, the resignation creating a thin glaze over his abject terror. He saw the emotionless disgust on his mother, the austere fury on his father. He felt all eyes in the room pierce his peripherals as they turned to Sebbie in needling curiosity. They were just celebrating, for fuck's sake. This world wasn't fucking *fair*.

The roadrunner sped off into the night as Vel skidded to a stop. It was the very same park that the crime scene had been staged against. Close to Sebbie's home. There, strung up to a telephone pole, was a body limp, naked save for a pair of boxers. Bloody. Most notably though, the harsh yellowed light shone off of a head stripped bare from alopecia.

"Sebbie," Vel breathed, "*Sebbie!*"

The blood poured from wounds that matched the ones Vel had woken up with. Some still had crude sticks twisted into his skin, sticks that moved with the haggard half-breaths of his best friend. Vel dashed forward and up the pole, feet perched on the rungs and arms wrapped around to where Sebbie's wrists were tied. Blindly Vel tried to free him, cheek pressed against Sebbie's head.

"C'mon, Seb," Vel said shrilly, "You're gonna be okay. You're gonna be okay, alright? You said you gotta get outta here, so you *gotta*,"

Sebbie responded with a wheeze of air from lungs half-drowned in blood. Something stung Vel deeper than skin. Not again. No, *no, not again. Not again.* His hands slipped on the bonds tying Sebbie to the pole. His eyes wouldn't have been any help even if he could see what he was doing. There was something in the way. They hurt. They were wet.

"*Sebbie,*" Vel begged, tightening his hold around him on the pretense to keep him warm. Keeping him warm would keep him alive. (So juvenile, he knew, and yet,)

"*Fuck,*" he muttered after he started to shiver, "*Fuck!*" Vel untangled himself from Sebbie's fading body, scrambling down to pull the brick phone out of his pocket. He paced frantically, unable to take his eyes off Sebbie.

"911, what's your—,"

"*My friend,*" Vel cried out, "My friend, at the park, he's *dying*, I need help!!"

It fell into a nightmare. The dispatcher walked him through the details they needed, and the mundanity of it was just as grounding as it was surreal. Vel watched as Sebbie stilled. The temperature wasn't freezing, but it was cold. Gooseflesh dotted his own skin. Where the blood had cooled felt raw and refrigerated. Vel shivered tenfold.

A car pulled up. Emergency services were right behind it. Vel stammered, turning around to see Sarge approach. Her eyes were trained to the boy lashed to the pole. Her expression betrayed nothing, but she only lingered long enough to determine the outcome before looking to the living. Namely, Vel.

In all his horror Vel didn't say anything. Sarge didn't either. She simply pulled off her windbreaker and wrapped it around his shoulders. That's when he broke, sobbing full-force as his bloodied hands slipped around the windbreaker's zipper. All his bravado, and for what—and Sarge knew it, too.

She left for a moment, he didn't hear why, and he turned to watch the emergency workers gingerly lower Sebbie down. Their faces were grim. Vel didn't know why he was watching anymore, but he couldn't stop.

"Called your tía." Sarge returned. Vel mustered the will to glance at her. He didn't find anything in her eyes. Her sympathy lied in her actions. Vel found himself standing next to where she had parked her car, watching the EMTs move slow and solemn. She did too. Perhaps, some hours later, Bosman would as well—recognizing one of the boys he recklessly risked the trajectory of his life for. Vel crumpled and buried his eyes in his hands. Moments later—he would've thought it was hours were it not for the fact that the sky remained the same inky black polluted with orange—Tía Gloria arrived and curled his tall frame into her arms. Into the car. And away.

He was afraid to know who had done it. He was terrified that whoever had knew Dom, knew him, knew more people. What if they had been the one that had allowed them to get set up in the first place—or knew how to? Was that rational? Did it matter? All he could do was curl up in the car, hugging the cold blood close to his body as he wept. If they hadn't been set up, none of this would've happened. If they hadn't been set up and this *had* happened, maybe Vel would've been filled with righteous anger to investigate, to dig, to fuck around and find out. Now, though, he just wanted to disappear.

This all happened to the despairing beat of his tía's voice. Sometimes she attempted to comfort him, sometimes the reality of what was going on enveloped her and she responded to his weeping with her own. She drove them back to the safety of their house, and upon entering Vel confessed that he was in pain, physical pain, and he took off his shirt. Then came the expected *¡Ay, Dios mío!* before he was whisked away to the bathroom where she pulled the first aid kit out again.

He stood just as patiently as before, canyons carved in his face from the tears. As she dutifully cleaned the blood away, however, he noticed that her emotive panic to the situation was fading. Insultingly, it was replaced with a vague smile, full of awe and pride. Her hands passed over his puffy skin, reverently cleaning the wounds of a long dead Saint. Discontent gurgled in his gut and with each cleansing sting of alcohol he let out a stronger and stronger hiss.

"Tía Gloria," Vel said, cautious but not enough to hide his brewing anger, "What if I was gay?"

"*Oh*, mijo," she cooed, pressing clean, soft gauze to the first wound, "Better gay than a Witch."

He hurt.

Vel refused to look at her. He further refused to speak even when she asked if he felt alright now, though that was more due to the tangling of sinew and heartbreak in his throat. Renewed tears sat on the borders of his eyes.

Numb, just like after the loss of his mother. At least he had consolation in Dom, but there was no Sebbie to push drawings into his arms to cheer him up. Basketballs were ruthlessly passed to him. No one poorly harmonized with his half-trained voice. A party member disappeared from their adventure. Movie nights ceased.

A little over a week later, students started walking out of class in protest, the one Cassidy Morello had told him about what seemed a lifetime ago. It was as good an excuse as any. Vel walked out of school and, avoiding his tía at home, drove mindlessly with music blasting in his car. He wanted to sing, but his voice rattled. He wanted to sing, but there was no one to harmonize with. He drove until the sky turned purple, turned black, enveloped the desert.

Vel had long driven out of the confines of the city, out into the wild winds where the blackness of the sky exploded into stars, untouched by manmade light. He could keep going. Out into lands where the stars still kissed the ground, where no one but the sun would know him, or Sebbie, or his mother. Out there he could start anew and forget everything that had ever happened to him—hell, he could make it all up if someone asked. Make himself cooler than he actually was, or, more likely, far more *normal* than he actually was. The fantasies knitted into a backstory; *my mom owned a gas station so I've always wanted to hoof it across the country and so now I'm doin' just that. Ain't much to it, I just had to put the foot to the pedal and go, go, go. And leave it all behind.*

Leave Tucson, leave his tía, leave all the blood spilled on the ground it seeped into. Ah, but if he lifted his foot from the pedal that same blood had stained the bottom of his shoes, tracked behind him wherever he walked. He could run forever but he couldn't outrun his skin. He could run forever, but Dom had too much to stay for in Tucson. Running would mean leaving Dom alone in his grief.

Vel had been there before. To force someone to go through the same thing would be the cruelest thing Vel could think to do. Worse, he *could* and *would* do it if he let himself, blinders on, driving on into the starry night.

Look at what Rita had done to his friends, done to herself! What about her sons?

So he drove home instead.

Less than four years later gay marriage became legal nation-wide, and Vel sat staring at the TV announcement with a hollow pain in his chest. He couldn't be sure that it would've saved Sebbie, he couldn't be sure it'd save future Sebbies. Maybe it would've helped. Maybe it *would* help. That was the last day he had ever listened to *American Idiot.*

Now that old disc, battered with age, use, and abandonment, rested against Sebbie's picture on his ofrenda.

19

The road had long become a suggestion. Gravel crunched and his tires slipped on dust. Red rimmed along the edges of his windshield from where he wiped away that dust. There was no sense pushing his poor sedan any more. Even if there hadn't been an old wooden fence marking the true end of the road he would've given in. It was the same car since high school, and Vel gave the dashboard a pat in gratitude. They had been here before.

It had been visible for a while now, a dark rusty smear on the horizon line. He'd felt it before he could truly see it, the vague austerity clouding the ground underneath a freer sky. According to his mother it had not always been like this. When he was very small it had just been chainlink, no flimsier than the stuff that kept kids on the school playground. It wasn't something she brought up often, though he did see the distant intensity in her expression when news would crackle on the radio. A border fence extension, more patrols, plummeting job economies attributed to immigrants, another semi-truck full of people found abandoned and cooked in the trapped heat. Vel set the emergency brake and stepped out, resting against the trunk of his car to stare at the border wall.

It was stupid, that's what it was. There were too many other words he could say, truly far too many things, but there was no way to. It wasn't polite, it was screaming into the void, it invited people to calm him down with platitudes that were skin deep. What could he say? It was a crusted scab over a deep wound that wasn't inflicted on his skin, not really, not at all—he'd never been to Mexico and didn't speak the language and didn't have connections nor plans to travel there. But on the other side of the fence were people who knew him in a way the average American wouldn't and that twisted him into perplexing shapes. Lullabies his mother would sing to him in gentle Spanish; sometimes folk songs, other times ranchera ballads that she and every other Mexican grew up with. Sometimes he wondered if the hospitality he felt from Dom's family would extend to him if he crossed the border, but then his tía's brutal words about the indio color of his skin would form a lump in his throat. What of the original people of the land, what did that say about him, how could he relate that deep? The wound wasn't on his skin. But he still felt it, a taut prickle, a scab to endlessly pick at, always in the back of the mind and occasionally rising to the surface.

Trying to articulate what he hoped to gain from talking about it or why he wasn't seeking comfort was more effort than it was worth. Here, at the end of October, after losing *another* loved one, all Vel wanted was to see the wall again.

He still couldn't put into words why. It was stupid.

It was stupid.

Distantly, he could hear the gravel crunching of the border patrol in their off-road SUVs. Strangely, gracefully, they were only ever distant sounds—kept away just for this. Above his head the sun had passed its zenith and was already becoming orange though it'd be several hours yet before sunset. The desert was hot. Vel pushed his hands into his pockets and barely noticed the breeze.

The gravel crunching gradually got louder, though from behind him. Vel turned his head, taking a moment to figure out if he should've been surprised that Lieu had taken her civilian car on the hour and a half trip to the border. Similarly, he raised eyebrows at her civilian clothes. He had seen her in her uniform so much it might as well be her skin, her regular clothes more akin to ballroom gowns even though all she was wearing was a simple heathered t-shirt and pants. He gave a short wave at her eye contact, and that was greeting enough for her.

"Are you looking for something specific?" Lieu asked.

"Sure am," Vel answered, "Two places. Not too much walking if I remember correctly. You got water?"

Lieu lifted up a hefty bottle dotted with condensation. He smirked in acknowledgment, then jerked his head in the direction of the border wall. It was more or less a straight shot from the end of the road, so due south from Tucson it made him shiver to think of it. Lieu followed behind him for the short trek to the wall proper.

"No patrols?"

"You say that like I did something," Vel pouted theatrically. He glanced back to see her eyebrow raise.

"Did you?"

"Yup!" he said as cheerfully as he could make it, "Put vinegar on like it was cologne."

She wrinkled her nose and he laughed. Lieu gave a curdled, "Oh."

Vel explained, "You ever want to sit down for a picnic or something so you circle your area with vinegar to ward off all the pests? *Or*, when the weather stripping is so shit in your house?"

Lieu was quiet for a moment, "No."

"So I figure, why not keep the pests off me for one day? Or for as long as it lasts before I sweat it off."

"Right." Lieu said with the deadened weight of someone who had been dealing with his bullshit explanations (that somehow worked) for eleven years.

Face-to-face with the fence, Vel raised a tentative knuckle then hesitated with a breath he didn't really want Lieu to hear. No, she wouldn't say anything. But still. With a spark that was more *fuck it* than *courage* he knocked on the rusty red metal. The tone was dull, hardly sing-song. He tapped on another bar, then another, all returning a similar tone. If this was part of the wall that was piled high with junky shipping containers he'd do more than just bang the drums on them. Though, he wasn't sure he'd be able to drum on them at all, too frightened that the returned sound would be silenced voices.

Lieu was quiet, watching him as though he was at work on a crime scene. Really he was delaying...something, he didn't know what. But when he tapped on a bar and it didn't return a noise to him he bit down on a nervous grin and peered through the bars.

Vel craned, willing his vision to parse the sloping land buried in brush and scrub with the occasional tree, "I think, that...it should be right here." He spoke, more to calm his anxiety than explain himself to Lieu. Still, that explanation had her curiously approach the fence and start peering in alongside him.

"What am I looking for?" she asked, unable to or unwilling to erase the dampened exasperation in her voice.

"Stone," Vel answered, "Pure white, if I remember correctly. You're looking for graves."

Lieu pulled away to look at him incredulously. Vel only gave her a glance. Then, before she could ask for actual clarification he chirped.

"*There!*" he jutted a finger between the slats, "Right there, hidden by the grass!"

Reluctantly, Lieu looked. As she did so Vel started seeing more of them, shapes too straight and constructed to be natural. White crosses, stone, metal, and maybe even wood stuck out from the cleared dirt. Though the graves were markers in it of themselves there was little else to mark the land that the graves *were* there, other than a bar of the border fence that did not sing when asked to.

"...I don't see it." Lieu said.

"Need a boost?" Vel asked, feeling the grin curl up his cheeks.

"No." she refused quickly and coldly.

"Wouldn't be any trouble," he exaggerated his politeness, making him think of his neighbors, "Just prop your feet in my hands, *or* I could give you a big hug—,"

"*No.*"

Vel chuckled but let her be, watching the breeze move the grass and branches just enough so that different flashes of white stone were visible. After a while he heard a huff of light frustration and Lieu gave up.

"What kind of graves?"

"Chinese," Vel answered, and in his peripherals he saw Lieu's body language recoil again in confusion. He didn't break his gaze, though, and kept speaking though his voice was going through the gaps in the wall, "Immigrants to Mexico from China. They weren't allowed to bury their dead with everyone else, so they found a spot here, east of Nogales," he perked up on his tip-toes, "Not a big destination spot either way."

"Right." Lieu said again, and the ensuing silence told him she was waiting to hear of why *this* place, how did *he* know about it when he'd never been to Mexico? For a moment Vel was pulled back. Lieu knew a lot about him but also not much at all, and he could say the same for her. Curling his fingers and imagining a world where he *didn't* tell her, Vel pressed a knuckle to the soundless bar of the fence and let it rest.

"My mom hid out there. Trying to cross the border." his hand slid, skin catching on the weathered and rough texture of the fence, "Wasn't trying to impose on holy ground or anything. Just out of options. And—," he swallowed.

Thought for a moment.

Continued, "The way she told it, the spirits of those buried there helped her cross all together."

He let that stand as is, knowing Lieu would not brazenly crave for details he didn't want to give. Sometimes that felt callous, other times generous. Standing and staring at the spot his mother cowered some 28 years ago Vel couldn't tell what it was.

It always struck him how exposed the graveyard looked. There was no safety to be had even if she tried to climb into the shrub-like trees that dotted the boundaries. What's more, she had never really detailed what had been hunting her. Coyotes, both literal and figurative? Mexican police? An angry mob comprised of irate locals? In the nightmares passed down to him from her stories he imagined it as all three at once, even if they weren't working together. A swelling hue and cry pushing her flat to the ground until she sprang out of it to the relative safety of namelessness in Arizona. Even at night under the cloudless desert sky those white graves would blaze in the moonlight—but such were the options of the desperate.

His mother had said there were whisperings in her ear, flowing like a river. It had frightened her terribly, interpreting the voices as the murmured weeping of La Llorona. But the more they spoke the more she recognized the flow of speech; questions, discussion, smatterings of Spanish amongst a language she didn't know. Attempts to communicate, even with some speaking with so heavy an accent she couldn't make out the words. Too afraid to whisper back she tried putting the words *por favor, por mi hijo* into the small bubbled world of the graves.

Then they were only speaking in the language she didn't know and she was frightened she had said the wrong thing. But then her limbs stretched and shrank. Her voice silenced in mercy. Before long she was running, fleeing, bounding past the white beams of flashlights to the Santa Cruz River.

Vel couldn't begin to guess as to why they had immigrated all the way to Mexico, nor why they had helped his mother in such a way. But maybe that was it; they had immigrated at best and fled at worst. Maybe in their hearts that now beat in the air instead of a chest they knew his mother in a way others didn't, couldn't. Just in that moment. In that desperation. From one immigrant to another, if not for a better life then at least a different one.

Vel liked to think it *had* been a better life for her.

They walked. For once Vel didn't fill the space with words, not even mundane ones. Every now and then though he'd raise a knuckle and tap the fence, following the ringing tones of the beating hearts that passed through the borders. One after the other. Many frightened, some of them hopeful, with papers or without. Before TUSD had ripped Mexican-American history from the curriculum he remembered seeing old maps of the

US–Mexico border. The line they followed, the wall they kept to their west, had not always been a border. So too did he have skin that didn't used to have scars. Pushing further back he wondered if there were borders no living person remembered; territorial disputes, trade routes, throngs of families traveling the land towards pueblos across all seasons. What that made of the earth they set their feet on now, Vel didn't know. He felt wistful, melancholy. Confused, yet too muffled to express that confusion.

When the river could be heard he saw a small tuft of fur stuck in the fence. Vel bent down, grateful for the break in his thoughts. It was the toe of a bobcat, its claw pinched into a joint in the slats that the animal couldn't figure how to undo. Despite its state of decay, he carefully pried it free and tucked the find into his pocket. Some day he'd find a use for it, as with all things he picked up from gauche branded snacks to animal remains. For the moment, he did not want to think about all the things a claw helplessly stuck in the border wall could remind him of.

The Santa Cruz River used to be louder. It was something he felt more than knew, gazing over at the struggling riverbed. Supposedly Pima County was working to help restore it with treated wastewater. He hoped that'd be enough. A jackrabbit could swim in it now, but not so camouflaged, not so part of the river as before. Still he paced the old bank where buds of thick grass held the memory of the river's original breadth.

"My mother was accused of being a Witch, you know." Vel said, knowing Lieu was there but speaking as though it was just him and the pages of a diary.

"I know." Lieu confirmed.

"She taught me a lot of things that I'm not sure were magic

or spiritual, religious or witchy, I don't know."

"How did that work?" she asked him. Vel pursed his lips, thinking hard.

"I don't think it was half as much what she said so much as how she thought about things. It wasn't that she passed down *water has memory, spit in a hand and make a lens to see someone's memories.*" he heard Lieu's breath short at the unexpected pull of their shared moment, not discussed since it happened, "It was more...Here's a way you can see the world. Like uh, building blocks. Not quite. Molecules of atoms? I don't know. But like a bad present, it's the thought that counts rather than the material the present is made out of."

Lieu didn't respond to any of that, and he supposed he wouldn't have had a response either.

"I miss her." he said bluntly. A chunk of grass dried from the recessed reach of the river gave way under the toe of his boot and he retreated just enough to watch it crumble into the smoothed sand of the old riverbed, "I wanted Laura to meet her so badly."

Lieu was silent, enough that he'd call it out of respect even though it was more likely she just knew there was nothing to say.

"She always seemed to know what to do," Vel continued, "Meanwhile I don't know a goddamn thing. And sometimes I feel like that gets people...well. It's not enough to save them." This time he pressed his boot into the sand just beneath the bank and found it softer than he expected, the texture clay-like from dampness he hadn't realized was there. Perhaps the river was growing back, even if only from concerted effort. But it didn't feel like enough.

"Every now and then I get so angry at her for dying. Uncontrollably. *How could she leave me alone?* I'm so angry, I love her so much, and she left me alone with so little to have." Red water splashed against the leather of his boots, lapping higher up his shins as he waded into the river, "Magic that I believe in but doesn't make me feel powerful. One language less than I should have. People to lose. What's one more, anyway?"

He tilted his head to the side, not quite glancing over his shoulder but enough to let Lieu know he wasn't a lost cause. She remained rooted on the bank, watching as water ate up his legs but never became a threat to his height. The last words he had ever said to his mother were *I don't care*. It was in response to being asked to clean his messy room. She had told him to do it, otherwise his titiritero will yank his strings tight and his limbs won't move again. (Tetanus, he deduced later in life.) Vel had rolled his eyes, his father's eyes, told her he didn't care, and left the house to explore. It had been dark by the time he had returned, water bottle and stomach empty. Her body was there, but she was gone.

Then Sebbie. Now Laura. Vel raised a foot out of the water, watching it drip off his heel before reaching for the far bank.

The trail to his mother's killer had gone cold. Any and all clues were walled off to him by rusty red bars. Why search for the person who killed a woman without documents to prove she lived there, lived anywhere? In the eyes of the wall-builders, it was the universe righting itself, like water leveling out between two containers. Even her own sister didn't seem concerned with finding who did it. By this point Vel lived by building his own peace with it.

Not that it was easy. Not that he felt like he had done it at all. But at the same time he had no idea how to be anybody else. To live with another person's life and history felt impossible, because everywhere he turned—English speakers, Spanish speakers, queer spaces, coworkers, neighbors, *something* felt off. *Something* always set him apart. One piece of his puzzle would fit with one group but not another, and there was never a place where all his pieces could fit together. Always, always, always there was the rusty red wall cutting right through him.

Vel sat on the bank opposite Lieu, facing the border wall. Not long after he pulled out a cigarette and lit it. Who would he have been if he was on the other side? If his mother hadn't fled, hadn't had *reason* to flee—if he spoke fluent Spanish and broken English, if he'd never met Dom and Sebbie, if he had never fallen for Laura. There'd be others in their spaces, certainly. Vel wanted to know who they would've been. Would he have lost them all the same, or would they have stayed in his life? In his wildest dreams his mother lived on the other side of that wall, content and unafraid. Maybe even his father was there too, though he didn't want to be selfish. He only wanted to be whole, and the grass looked so much greener on the other side.

But he had decided long ago not to abandon a home half-built, and until Laura came back from the dead it was destined to forever be half-built. For as much as his heart ached an ancient pain looking at the wall, Tucson was the home of his body and his blood. Blood he held in his hands. Blood spilled by his mother, his best friend, and his lover, all soaking the earth, all staining the land with his handprints on their cold bodies.

"I miss them so much." he said aloud. Lieu heard it even if it was distant, likely heard it like he had said it into her ear. His body spoke it as much as his voice did. From across the riverbank she spoke, emotionlessness cracked with concern.

"Are you going to be okay?"

Vel shrugged, taking another drag of the cigarette, "No other way to be." No other way he knew how to be. Lieu stood and watched him smoke with the sun dipping overhead, soon to be something redder and purpler than before. Vel gazed out, disappearing from the present. So too did the wall, just for a mere miraculous moment. He wasn't fooled, knowing it was there, knowing that by now it would be there for years to come even if he tore it down right here and now. Vel pressed a hand to his chest and rubbed it, feeling the fabric catch on Saint Sebbie's blunt scars. There, visible for everyone to see if they got close enough to look. There, even if they completely healed over, in Vel's mind forever.

He snuffed the cigarette in the riverbank and took the butt with him. Lieu watched him wade back across, and they followed the wall back to their cars.

"Ah, shit," Vel swore. A border patrol SUV was wedged between their two cars with an officer closely inspecting them. Falling behind Lieu, Vel all but pushed her ahead to cover him. He could still smell the vinegar on the back of his neck, but in hindsight that meant its warding followed *him* and did nothing for his car.

"Hello," the officer greeted, friendly in a way that was heavily guarded, however they pulled *that* paradox off, "These vehicles belong to you folks?"

"Yes." Lieu answered flatly, pulling out her badge when they were close enough for him to see it. Vel stayed silent, unscrewing the cap of his water bottle to busy himself with hydration instead of talk.

"Tucson," the officer whistled, "What are you doing way down here?"

"He wanted to see the border wall."

"Did he, now?" the officer's eyes wandered over to him. *Goddammit Lieu.*

"My mom remembered when it was just a chain link fence. Wanted to see how much it changed."

It was unclear if the officer was buying it or not, catching the unspoken truths in the smaller one, "Didn't bring her along with?"

"Oh I did. Was spreading her ashes." Vel said casually, shaking his water bottle that was very clearly full of liquid. Liquid he had just taken a big swig of. At this the officer raised an eyebrow quizzically, and Vel took small joys in seeing the wheels turn in his head. Hell, he wouldn't even mind if the officer wondered if he drank the ashes to piss them out. What food for thought. Why not piss on the fence anyway, and rot it from the blood-soaked earth up?

He bit his tongue. This was why he brought Lieu along.

"Strange place to be spreading ashes." the officer commented.

"She was a strange woman." Vel said, meant that to be it, then couldn't help himself from adding, "I loved her."

For once, that seemed to help his case. The officer gazed at him, then looked back at Lieu's badge. Lieu gave a single nod in support of his words, and the officer did not know them well enough to know that she only supported half his words half the time. An air of suspicion still surrounded him, but he packed it away for if they were to be repeat offenders and let them go.

Vel paused before getting in his car, giving the border wall one last look. Lieu spoke freely then, and he caught the disbelief in her voice. Disbelief that he *wanted* to be here at all, unable to understand why it could've been important.

"Did it help?"

Once more, Vel shrugged, "I think I would've regretted it if I didn't come down here."

Lieu did not understand and he knew it. But it was answer enough, and they got into their cars to leave.

20

The haircut felt as refreshing as it was alienating. A return to a normal he couldn't fool himself to feel, but at least it'd keep Tía Gloria from smothering him. He knocked on her door, now a smidge shorter than he was. He could've just entered without announcing himself; it was well accepted if not welcomed. But there was a barrier between them.

A handful of years ago, around the time he was realizing just how serious his relationship with Laura was becoming, Vel and his tía had fought. Fought *hard*, too. Of course by now Vel had forgotten exactly what was said, but he remembered the whys. It was very hard to forget the whys, even if just in emotion. The years of frustration piling into the realization that he felt betrayed by his aunt, betrayed she called herself aunt, betrayed that she took him in without real complaint—except for the fact he'd been born at all, since she still denied him the birthright of having parents even in just remembrance. She cared about a nephew, but it wasn't clear that she cared about *him*.

Now, she must've remembered the fight too, but it was unclear if she suppressed the whys. She at least suppressed bringing it up for the sake of welcoming him back into the rectangular home, still opulent with worship and filled with the scent of food. He had seen her from time to time since the fight but had never stayed long enough to slip the car keys from his hand until now. The overwhelming energy of her voice said she was thinking of that too, ushering him inside with a smile and her arms around his skinny waist.

"Jeró! Are you eating?? Come in, sit, sit! You need to be fatter! You can't be a walking skeleton!!"

"Oh, I figured today of all days would be the day to dress up like a pile of bones," he retorted, the glum reality plain in his voice despite the humor of his words, "Hey, Tía."

"*Hey Tía*," she huffed indignantly, smacking his chest as she retreated, "That's all you can say?! *Hey Tía?!*"

"Left my lust for life in my other coat," he said, then followed up with, "Also lust's a sin, ain't it,"

"*Ay!* The way you live it's all a sin!" she scoffed and turned towards the kitchen.

"Don't tempt me," he teased, "I can do worse."

Another scoff, this time flatter with the weight of disappointment behind it. The weight of a door cracked ajar just enough that the light from the other side got through, and it was not a light he particularly wanted to see, "You started smoking again."

"Sure did," he replied like he was talking to her about the weather, "Call me crazy but I think it's addicting."

"Sí, estás loco."

Well at least we can still agree on that, Vel thought, then bit back his tongue. He didn't want to start something today, and despite the door hanging ajar in her voice he could tell she didn't either.

And then there was a deep pang in his chest, a frustrated wail of hurt when he wanted to tell her *it's been hard. It's been so hard, Tía,* and he felt it so strongly that he wanted to cry on the spot. Cry, because he couldn't tell her, couldn't trust her with that information. If she responded with sympathy it'd feel hollow no matter how sincere—always for her own betterment rather than learning what he wanted because what he wanted was painted as juvenile anyway. *Better than a Witch.*He couldn't decide if it would be worse to receive a lecture from her instead, even if she implied he was dumb to the world and always would be. He'd be one year away from thirty in two months, and the more she kept treating him like an idiot child into his adult years the easier it was to discard such lectures as ignorant. Now, he didn't want to shirk that he would always have something to learn (it'd kneecap his abilities as an investigator for one) but he wanted to be treated as though he *had* learned. He wanted his tía to accept him as one of her own; nephew, yes, but an adult one.

For now, he settled with *estás loco.*

Vel at least acknowledged her with one huff of laughter and wandered into the living area while she plated up food. There was an ofrenda set up directly in front of the TV, restricting the space to move. As he remembered, it had a photograph of his buelita whom he had never met and even a photograph of Sebbie as her attempt to meet him at his grief. Likewise, there was a new photograph placed on the altar; a large, silver, ornate frame encircling Laura. It was the same one set into the simple wooden frame he had constructed for his own, yet it looked so different when wreathed with over-complicated filigree. He didn't exactly *like* that his frame was so simple, of course, but he wouldn't have personally chosen this frame for her either.

Well. At the same time, Vel had to take solace in the fact that Laura would've delighted in both, vocally, too. Any expression extended at all had been a precious one to her, just as indicative of the gift-giver as the receiver. Tía Gloria had chosen this frame because she had known he had loved Laura, that she had been the best thing that had ever happened to him. She was *important*. After years of denying most everything else, it was...it was enough. For now.

Cold touched his arm and he looked down to take the offered beer from his tía. As he did so she spoke, "She was good. You know. Very nice. Liked asking questions."

"She liked how people answered," Vel said. Tía Gloria had already turned back to the kitchen. She had heard him, certainly, the space was too small to pretend otherwise. But the precision in Vel's words, the implication of why he loved her and how she thought, saw people, loved them back, *that*, that was lost on his tía. Vel sank into the couch as she began to regale a memory of Laura, specifically the time when she had asked a question about how saints worked in Catholicism. This meant that it was not really a memory of Laura; beyond her being the catalyst it was nothing more than Tía Gloria recounting the saints to him, again. From the saints she prattled into offshoots of how they intervened in the lives of nun sisters she once knew, sometimes by second or third hand.

Laura was good. She had not lied. Vel felt his body tangle in the couch even as she brought a plate of mole chicken to him. Laura was good, good, so good. Good enough to earn a place on his tía's ofrenda.

Unlike his mother.

He had a memory of gripping his mother's hand, at her hip when he was much much shorter than everyone else. Every other time the grip had been warm, even deferring, but when he was with her to confront Tía Gloria, well. Her hands became hard, as if there was no fat nor skin to cushion her bones. Vel had always remained silent without complaint, and looking back he believed that she didn't even realize she had been doing it.

His buelita had passed. It took years of reflection to notice the subtle ways that Tía Gloria implied it was his mother's fault; causing stress and heartbreak until it overloaded the poor woman. Now they were left with dealing with the remnants of her belongings and an estate on the other side of a border his mother couldn't—wouldn't—cross again. To say that complicated things was an understatement. Then Tía Gloria complicated it more by barring her from owning any of the belongings they *did* have, declaring them for charity via the Church before she could even look at them. It had been a similarly brutal fight to the one he'd have with his tía decades later where he didn't remember the words as much as the tension.

At one point his mother's hand left his as she turned away to—cry? He still didn't know. Tía Gloria had pressed—what else—but a gloria candy into the palm of his small hand. Confusion swarmed his mind as he unwrapped it and took careful bites as though it was the size of a sandwich. If he wasn't convinced it was poison, the sweet caramelized treat tasted rather like nothing. Then his mother turned around, skirt hiked up into her hands and she ushered him out the door. She was quiet in a way he wasn't used to, her eyes red and her jaw set tight and solemn. But she pulled a smile out of the darkness when they had gotten home, showing him that she had managed to steal away his buelita's VHS tapes of old Mexican movies.

Vaguely he wondered if his tía ever noticed they were missing, and if she surmised it was their fault, how long it had taken her to make the decision to never confront them about it. She sat on the opposite end of the couch with her own plate, and Vel gazed sidelong at her. She looked so much, and so different, than her sister. Allowed to deny things. Allowed to age. Allowed to be mean in a way his mother couldn't afford without citizenship—with the ever-growing wall between borders, between them. Allowed, above all other things, to raise him.

"Tía Gloria," he said, suddenly direct even if his voice was calm, piercing through the gaps of her words to cut her short, "Thank you."

It was deliberately sincere in both its bitterness and its truth. The way she paused in response, meeting his sidelong stare with her own, yes, she scrutinized the sudden gratitude. As she should. She was stubborn, but not dumb, and what's more she *knew* him. *Knew* their relationship, for its craggy rocks barely keeping their shape together over dizzying pitfalls.

Vel looked away to where his mother might've rested on the ofrenda if there had been any space made for her and took a swig of beer. At least some part of his tía, no matter how deeply she buried it, couldn't lie to herself about him.

Maybe it was the holiday, maybe it was the deep grief emanating from him, but she let the moment of high guard pass, filling her voice with warmth that he associated with burning, corralling, branding. It was safe to be branded. She had provided for him in her corral. And she had burned him.

"Of course, mijo. You're welcome to any time."

Wordlessly, he took another swig of beer.

* * *

There was something golden about the streets of Tucson as he drove home, or maybe it was the dust in the air. Or maybe it was the dust that was golden anyway.

Or maybe it was the dust that was golden anyway.

The house was just as empty as the day before, and the day before that, and before, and so on into the bleak days of the past summer. Strangely in the house's quiet what he missed the most was when he and Laura would get into an argument. Ones that would end so fierce she'd shut herself behind a slammed door and blast music so loud he'd feel it through his feet on the other side of the house. Sometimes he'd be pissed that it was her music at all, but it was often so loud it was hard to think; paradoxically shutting the rest of the world away while he calmed down. When he was calm enough he'd start singing along. Softly, at first. Until he got louder and louder, and though he didn't consider himself a serious singer he knew how to carry the quality of his voice to stand with and above the music. Then he would notice that Laura would ever so slightly lower the volume to hear him better, so he'd keep singing. Sooner rather than later the door would open and Laura would shuffle out, sometimes sheepishly wrapping her arms around his waist to feel him inhale deep into his belly for the notes. Sometimes she'd rest wearily against him. Whatever it took to quietly tell him she was okay, they were okay, they were always going to be okay.

His office, with his own ofrenda, was dark. Lighting it with candles made it golden, the rich warmth seeping into everything including the bright colors of his baby blanket. The photographs on the ofrenda came alive with it; sunlight on Sebbie's bald head, laughing blush on Laura, and life, life in his mother.

Remember, Momo, he spoke to himself in a way that didn't feel like he was speaking to himself. The crackle of the poor sound of old films sputtering on the VCR, remember how she translated the movies on the fly without complaint, the confusion on whether this helped or hindered his ability to speak Spanish. How little he was, unaware of much of the world when he thought that Pedro Infante's swagger under a wide sombrero was what a hero looked like, remember the voiceless confusion as he slowly learned to stifle it when others regarded it as caricature at best, ugly at worst. Remember how she pet your hair back and you wondered if never learning Spanish was protection, protection that was important and painful but protection all the same.

Vel slumped on the pull-out couch, wishing the one person who called him Momo would do so again. Lots of remembering, very little calling. He gazed at Laura's picture in the amateur wooden frame he had made.

"I think the worst part," he spoke into the candlelit room, "Is that you two would've loved each other."

His gaze turned to his mother, perched on the covered copy of *The Canterbury Tales* that had belonged to Laura, "You would've loved her."

Vel, Jeró, Momo felt his large frame grow heavy and droop over the edges of the couch.

"Well," he muttered to himself, "I guess you've figured that out by now, anyway."

He closed his eyes. There was a slight chill to the air, comfortable in its briskness as it embraced the lifting warmth from the desert. Vel opened his eyes and found himself staring at a door he hadn't seen in almost two decades. His instinct was to pull it open, duck under the low height and enter because he was always going to be welcome to. Keeping that instinct under his tongue, Vel raised his knuckles and politely knocked. Night buzzed quietly around him.

And then his mother opened the door, his eyes blurring to the point where he could barely make her face out from the throng of emotion. Vel's heart had known it'd be her, but that knowledge was disconnected from his mind and in their clashing he tried to stifle his own weeping.

"Mom," he choked, "Can I come in?"

She smiled and said, "Of course, Momo," with such natural warmth it was odd. It was a wonder why she didn't question him or seem perturbed by this full grown man claiming to be her son when her son was, at best, her height. Vel was so, so much taller now, towering over her as he had to fold into the tiny door to enter the home.

Immediately the soothing scent of chamomile settled deep into his throat, and he followed his mother to its source in the tiny kitchen. Vel took in the rest of the house, trying to put a time to this place by judging the photos on the wall, if the carpet yet had a stain from where he dropped a soda, if she had yet gotten better blankets for her makeshift bed on the couch, if the colors of the curtains were brighter than his last memory of them.

"Are you...," he drew his eyes to her again, her chin tilted down to tend to the chamomile boiling on the stove. He had never seen her from a higher angle before, and so much of her face was hidden from him because of it, "Are you alright?"

"Yes," she answered, bringing the wooden spoon discolored from years of stirring hot pans to her lips, "But you're sick, in your room."

Vel looked past the humble living room to where his door was ajar. From within he saw the old familiar glow of his lamplight, but it didn't flicker with the shadows of an energetic child. More pieces fit together, and Vel surmised he was about nine, ill with the flu on an early fall night.

"I wouldn't go in there," his mother cautioned, the tone of her voice commanding in her quiet, subtle way. Like she was telling him to not touch the stove or to not rely on the fickle nature of magic. But there was a softness to it because she trusted him. She seemed to have always trusted him appropriately.

Vel shook his head and brought his mind back to the kitchen, "I...I'm tired, Mom."

"You look tired."

"Yeah," he mumbled, watching the water in the dutch oven boil. Part of him craned his neck to try and make out the herbs she was stirring into the chamomile, but apart from the stray recognizable flower bud he couldn't make out anything. The more she stirred the more he realized that it was *impossible* to make out; something clouded either his vision or his understanding, keeping her recipe forever locked away. It almost felt like death in its stubborn finality. His brows pinched together, "Do you...know what happened?"

"No," she said, almost blissfully. That *bliss* seemed to come from an understanding that she wasn't supposed to know, and the *almost* came from the darkness of knowing that some things happened in the world that were just beyond anyone's control.

"I miss you," he said, whispered and pathetic as the little boy that lost her unfurled in his chest, "I miss...everything."

"You're here now," his mother answered, "What would you like to do?"

Vel stood there, pondering the question as the water boiled in mystery. Over the many years of loss he had played out many a fantasy in his head. Certainly there were ones of miraculous justice, even revenge, but they paled in number to the ones where he simply got to have one last *something* with someone. Another after-school moment with Sebbie, another argument with Laura, just one more meal with his mother. But as he stood there he found he wanted for nothing, could conjure nothing even as the offer was so freely given to him. Vel found that he didn't particularly want to *do* anything.

"I don't know," he said, a dull pain throbbing behind his eyes. He gave a small laugh, "I guess I don't know at all."

She allowed for a pause, stirring the chamomile tea as it darkened to a toasted gold color.

Vel stuttered, "I just want things to be okay, again."

"Again?" she asked, the question far more probing than a single world should've had any right to be.

He made a strange noise in his throat, struggling to answer her, "I think...I'm, I'm never going to love again. I'm scared I'll never love again."

"You won't," she said, gentle, "No, you won't ever love like that again."

Vel's words stuck in his throat.

"Whatever love you will find will be different. No love is the same, from person to person, yes?"

"Sí," he said, blinking because he didn't understand what about her cadence compelled him to respond in Spanish.

"It's good that it will never be the same," she continued, "A person dies, and all of what they are goes with them. And the love that you felt for them can't be for someone else, because that's *their* love, too."

When he didn't (couldn't) respond, she continued.

"When you say you want things to be *okay, again*—do you mean you want to be here, again?"

In the middle of her words a weak groan pitched from behind the bedroom door, and his mother quickly and deftly scooped ladles of the tea into a mug. The groan mounted in its illness, becoming despairing as he heard his voice as a child call for her. Vel waited patiently as his mother turned in a flourish of her dress, carefully easing the door open before disappearing inside. He heard, quite clearly thanks to the small house, her cooing to him and remembered how she would cradle his feverish head at the neck. He remembered how she blew on the tea before she pressed it to his lips, and with the realization that it had been boiling mere seconds ago marveled at whatever control she had because the tea had never burned him. All the while he fought the urge to crane his neck to see these things from an outsider's viewpoint. No, he wanted to see it from *her* perspective. He wanted to know what she thought as she gazed at him, his brown skin beaded with sweat and his eyelids heavy over the color she attributed to his father. How she looked at him and loved her son, despite everything from the whole world to her very sister insisting on some inherent wrongness to her. The undocumented, the Witch, cupping her son's chin and wiping away the spilled chamomile as she nursed him back to health.

She soon returned without the mug, having entrusted it to his bedside table under the lamp.

"I don't know," he rasped, answering her earlier question, "But...,"

"Yes?" her ears were perked but patient.

"I want to help," he answered weakly, "I want to help people. I can't prevent...anything from happening. But I want to help, even if it doesn't."

She was quiet. She was quiet for so long Vel picked up that her thoughts were racing—though to where or what he couldn't know. He saw her shoulders tense as though he had threatened to harm her, then release with such a deeply relaxed sigh he couldn't believe it was anything but gentle pride.

"Oh, Momo," she said with a longing that did not hide the pain, "You've grown *very* tall."

She blinked, something so natural he shouldn't have been drawn to it. But it was for the first time then that he realized she had no eyes to begin with. There was only the deep dark of the hollows left behind, bloodless in their emptiness. Pain struck him then, deep in the chest. The pain of knowing, of watching her unfold before him in a way he could not control. She moved as though she had no wherewithal of her eyelessness, yet when she looked at him he felt as though she both knew and didn't know her fate at the same time.

"I love you, Mom," he murmured, staring at the hollows.

"I love you too." she responded, her steadfast refusal of Spanish making the words sound clumsy in their sincerity. Or maybe he had been around Tía Gloria too much, expecting her *y yo también*, and the severance between them never felt so tangible even so deep in this dream.

When Vel awoke it was as jarring as not remembering getting home from a night out drinking. He didn't remember leaving his old house, he didn't remember saying good-bye to his mother nor embracing her in a hug which he suddenly regretted he didn't do. Vel rubbed his eyes, groaned at the crick in his neck, and slumped halfway off the pull-out couch.

To bed, for the rest of the night.

And in the morning, he'd be okay, again.

Afterword

In the dark winter of 2011 it happened.

Not as gruesome. He lived—though sometimes I think about how close he came to not. They attacked him from behind, calling him a faggot and beating his face in until he passed out in a January snowbank. It was night. He was walking home from grabbing McDonald's.

I didn't know him. I still don't. But my brother did. He told me the day after he broke his leg on the ice, his foot perched up as he grimaced with pain, out of reach of his charging cell phone. The TV was on a channel he had decided on for once. For as long as our father wasn't in the room, he could blast RuPaul in whatever spite he could muster because it had not been a good week.

I still remember it like it was only a month ago, even though I was 17 at the time and comparatively naive. I remember feeling awful that I had gone to bed a mere twenty minutes before my brother limped home. I remember sitting with him the day after, taking in the fact that one of his friends was attacked in the town my brother worked nights in. It's something that has always felt very...quiet. If it showed up in the news, if it had an investigation, a conclusion, a closure...I don't know, and I'm almost certain it didn't.

There are many stories like this, hidden in the cracks, remembered only in private moments sitting together and sharing such news. They continue to be told to this day.

I don't feel right using that story as inspiration, even if it feels good to say "No, he survived, he lived, he needed facial reconstruction surgery but he lived. He woke up in the bloodied snowbank and dragged himself home." I wonder still if there's someone he used to look like but doesn't anymore. I wonder if his face holds a stiff uncanniness to it that he can't shake, and I wonder if that's from the surgery or the trauma of it all to begin with. All I know is when I first heard the news I could only think *but he's with us. He's my people.* It could've been my brother, but it didn't have to be—this man who was attacked was already my brother, in a way.

This book was in no small part how confusing it was to come of age in a time after 9/11, after Matthew Shepard. Before Sandy Hook, before marriage equality. To comfortably have friends that knew I was bisexual at school, only then to sit in that mid-morning with my brother, not knowing what to say—only knowing there was little that we could do. We were just glad he was alive.

I'm glad we're alive.

About the Author

Bre Garcia can't listen to *Cloudbusting* by Kate Bush without crying, can make her buelita's enchiladas without asking for the recipe, can't hold a conversation in Spanish, can write a book, can't think of anything else to say.

Also by Bre Garcia

Jackrabbit and the Beast